■ □ ■ □ ■

THE SECOND BOOK

Writings from an Unbound Europe

MUHAREM BAZDULJ

THE SECOND BOOK

Translated from the Bosnian

NORTHWESTERN UNIVERSITY PRESS

EVANSTON, ILLINOIS

Northwestern University Press
Evanston, Illinois 60208-4170

Printed in the United States of America

10 9 8 7 6 5 4 3 2 1

ISBN 0-8101-1935-8 (cloth)
ISBN 0-8101-1936-6 (paper)

A Note on the Translation
This book was translated in a somewhat unorthodox manner. Initial translations were produced for two of the stories by Nikola Petković and the rest by Oleg Andrić. Andrew Wachtel then revised all of the translations, which were sent to the author for his comments and approval.—A.W.

Library of Congress Cataloging-in-Publication data are available from the Library of Congress.

The paper used in this publication meets the minimum requirements of the American National Standard for Information Sciences—Permanence of Paper for Printed Library Materials, ANSI Z39.48-1992.

■ □ ■ □ ■

CONTENTS

■ □ ■ □ ■

THE SECOND BOOK

■ □ ■ □ ■

TEARS IN TURIN

Shame.—*A beautiful horse stands there, scratches the soil, wheezes, and longs for someone to ride it and loves the one who usually rides it—but, oh, what a shame! Today he is not able to soar on the horse, being tired.—That is a shame of a tired philosopher faced with his own philosophy.*

The Dawn

There are cases in which we are like horses, we psychologists, and become restless: we see our own shadow wavering up and down before us. A psychologist must turn his eyes from himself to eye anything at all.

Twilight of the Idols

12.31.1888

Just as the sun began to draw golden hieroglyphs on the wall through the translucent fabric of the curtains, Nietzsche woke up. The bed was under a window, so Friedrich, lying on his side, was able to observe undisturbed the golden symbols' dance on the white wall across from the window, a dance that reminded him of the flickering of Midsummer's Eve fires. In the silence he heard only the uniform sound of his own breathing and the slow and regular beating of his heart (as always, his pulse was never more than sixty beats per minute, just as it usually was never less than that limit; his heart beat exactly once per second like some atomic clock, the temporal equivalent of one of those geometric bodies of exact dimensions made of a particular alloy that are kept in a special institute as prototypes of official measurement units; thus if one kilogram is in fact the mass of an equilateral cylinder of a radius of thirty-nine millimeters made of an alloy of 90 percent platinum and 10 percent iridium kept in the International Bureau for Measurements and Weights in Sevres, then one second is the time during which Nietzsche's heart made one beat, and not, as it is claimed, the duration of 9192631770 periods of radiation corresponding to the transition between two hyperfine levels of the ground state of the cesium 133 atom—if this means anything at all). With his right hand he was massaging his forehead around the temples. Maybe he had a headache. Last night, as usual, he was bothered by insomnia, which almost every night was as quietly and unpretentiously persistent as the sound of a fountain. It returned eternally. That is why this morning, too, Nietzsche was lying wide awake and trying, apparently, to give his tired body a rest, a rest his brain did not want. It was as if his brain had an inkling of the rest it would not give his body. On a night table next to the bed were books stacked in straight towers, like floors of a high-rise. The letters on their spines formed some strange crossword, with the vertical letters making incomprehensible and mostly unpronounceable piles of consonants mixed with a few vowels, while the horizontal letters proffered the famous names of Dostoyevsky, Seneca, Stendhal, Kant, Thucidydes, Schiller, Heraclitus, Rousseau, Goethe, and Schopenhauer. On a desk by the wall, illuminated by the sun, were Nietzsche's papers and writings. He had written a lot in the past year, a year whose last hours were just passing. He had never liked this holiday, this so-called New Year, the grotesque tail of Christmas, *dies nefastus,* a day that in fact represents the day of the circumcision of the purported Messiah, his almost grotesque first spilling of blood. But today's day was nearly special even according to Nietzsche's personal calendar, the calendar he had invented in *The Antichrist* (which was on the desk among other writings), completed exactly three months ago, on September 30, 1888, according to—as he wrote—the false calendar. That day Nietzsche declared to be Salvation Day, the first day of the first year, making this thirty-first day of December of 1888 the second day of the third month of the first year. Nietzsche frowned while the thoughts of some mystic quasi-pythagorian analogy were probably going through his head. In fact, the day dearest to Friedrich, which he would pick as a starting point for his calendar (from which he—it is completely logical—did start counting time in a way), was his birthday—October 15. That day was in some way his name day—luckily, not in a religious sense. October 15 was the birthday of the Prussian king Friedrich Wilhelm IV after whom Nietzsche was named. On the desk among the manuscripts, as a silent witness, his *Ecce Homo* was lying. Nietzsche probably knew by heart all the sentences he had written not so long ago. Maybe he was whispering them now in his bed. *As I was born on October 15, the birthday of the above-named king, I naturally received the Hohenzollern name* Friedrich Wilhelm. *There was at all events one advantage in the choice of this day: my birthday throughout my entire childhood was a public holiday.* If Nietzsche was really remembering his childhood birthdays, when he believed that his whole homeland was celebrating just his birthday, then he could not have missed an ironic detail connected to his birthday and the calendar he had established three months ago that had declared September 30 Salvation Day and the start of a new calculation of time. By establishing his own calendar he had made himself a kind of Julius Caesar (and he loved Caesar as can be witnessed by another of his works, *Twilight of the Idols,* lying on the desk between *The Antichrist* and *Ecce Homo*). Caesar's calendar was adjusted approximately fifteen days backward by Pope Gregory, but if Nietzsche's calendar could be adjusted, this could be done only by some antipope and Antigregory, and adjusted in the only possible way, fifteen days ahead, making New Year's day fall on his birthday—the Antichrist's birthday, instead of some Middle Eastern mess about the circumcision of a purported Messiah. Nietzsche smiled silently. In moments of silence and loneliness he always found most similar to himself the personalities he scorned the most in his writings, the personalities of the two greatest and most famous oral teachers (and that was probably their only feature completely opposite to his own, because Nietzsche was a *teacher* only in a written sense, but orally—while teaching at the University—he was only a lecturer; but even this difference between the oral preaching of his two greatest *impossibles* and his own leaning toward written prophecies was more a consequence of the times than their characters): with the dialectician and the *rabbi,* Socrates and Christ. He raised himself on his elbows just to reach a clock on the night table with books, to see the time. It was almost eleven. But still, Nietzsche lay down again. Forgetting, apparently, that he had awakened at daybreak, he thought it might have been noon already, making this late morning moment too early for getting up. If he had already resigned himself to wait for noon in bed, then there was no reason not to do it. Again he smiled gently, as if he remembered that Russian novel in which the hero wakes up at the beginning of the novel and spends the whole first section lying lazily in bed. But Friedrich was not accustomed to lazy lying in bed. It must have been that some strange and undefined weakness enveloped him this morning, this day actually, because he was still prone even at half an hour after noon. But realizing the time, he immediately got up. Strangely, he was not hungry. He spent the next three hours—almost till dusk—sitting in a chair. This way his afternoon was the same as his morning, apart from his back being in a vertical position. Luckily, it was not cold although it was December. Such was Turin. (*The quiet and aristocratic city of Turin*—so he wrote in *Ecce Homo*.) When dusk fell in his room, Nietzsche decided to go out. The decision to eat something was more the fruit of his giving in to habit rather than to demands from his belly, his brain searched for food more than did his stomach. After having a quick meal, Nietzsche walked through the streets of Turin for a long time. Almost paradoxically, his tiredness diminished as he walked more. A light southern wind was bringing a puff of additional warmth to the already mild air, like the feeling of a burst of blood to the head of a man with fever. Nietzsche's forehead was beaded with sweat. But his heart was still working like a clock (and this comparison should not be considered colloquial but rather concrete and the most correct possible), and his breathing was just slightly quicker. At a street corner he stopped for a bit. He did not pause to rest (he didn't need to), nor because he was in thought (in his youth he had read somewhere that people with lower mental capabilities are incapable of thinking and walking at the same time, the start of any barely significant thinking stops them immediately; then with pleasure he remembered a fact he had noticed long ago, although without assigning to it any positive or negative meaning, the fact that he thought better and quicker while walking), he simply tried to separate the sensations of time and space, to put himself under the control of time while being motionless in space, as if by doing this the power of time over him would be higher, as if the sum of time and space within a person is always constant, bringing him closer to time if he gives less control to space, and vice versa. Then he went to a particular spot, *his own spot* on the banks of Po. He had gone there for the first time when he completed *The Antichrist,* on the first day of the first year of his own calendar. For the last three months he had been coming here almost every time he went walking. He watched the water flowing. A river by day is not the same as by night. The sound of a river flowing in darkness is unreal and healing. He came back home fifteen minutes after ten o'clock and went straight to bed. Usually he went to bed later, trying to trick the insomnia. But this time he lay down early and, amazingly, fell asleep quickly. He did not want to be awake to hear the clock strike *twelve irrevocable chimes.*

1.1.1889

The first morning of the New Year was well under way when Nietzsche woke up. Amazed, he rubbed his sleepy eyes, trying to remember the last time he had slept this well, so deeply and for so long. It was almost ten o'clock. This time his body did not desire lazy lying but immediate rising. Nietzsche got up and began measuring the room with his steps, as if merely standing was not enough but rather it was necessary to emphasize his alertness and the pleasure caused by refreshing sleep. He yawned not in the nighttime but in the good-morning way, which expresses not sleepiness but ultimate escape from the gluey fingers of sleep—these two facial grimaces are identical, but identical in the same way that in ancient Egypt a hieroglyphic symbol could represent two diametrically opposite things. This was a good beginning to January, almost like the one that a few years back gave him *The Gay Science.* To that January he had dedicated a poem in which he thanked it for *crushing the ice of his soul with a flaming spear.* Maybe this would be a similar January. *Each month has its own special and direct, weather-independent influence on our bodily condition, even on the condition of our soul.*—Somewhere sometime he had read this forceful diagnosis, which he accepted as correct even before it proved itself a few times in his life. Even his intimate calendar almost did not disturb the internal structure of months. With a new beginning came a new sequence of months, but some natural events, such as the beginnings of the seasons, still fell around the twenty-second of the month, just as in the *false calendar.* He stopped in the middle of the room almost out of breath. Walking in the room exhausted him, like a long walk in his cage exhausts a tiger. Then he opened a window and breathed good morning southern Piedmont air for a long time. The climate had always had a strong influence on his health and mood, and, consequently, on his writing. Who knows what would have happened to him had he always lived in his homeland, up there in the Teutonic cold? Good air makes a person feel fed and watered. This morning even the sky cheered up Nietzsche: clear, blue, bright, and crowded with birds. Leaving the window open, Nietzsche turned toward the interior of the room. He was looking at his desk. At the desk's edge lay sorted manuscripts of his completed works, and the rest of the heavy wooden surface was messily covered in handwritten papers with sketches of aphorisms and conceptual writings. They were lying there in heaps, more like fallen tree leaves than like leaves of paper, like an illustration of the magnificent Wordsworth-Huxley misunderstanding, that tragic and symbolic *meprise,* which occurred when Huxley, for the title of a novel, took a phrase Wordsworth had used in a poem in which he invited a friend into the bosom of nature, calling on him to forget about those barren leaves of old books; Huxley, therefore, named his novel *Barren Leaves,* but in its translation into foreign languages the novel is just about always called *Barren Tree Leaves.* But the unrelenting perfect linearity and continuity of time (despite its eternal return that confirms it, since a circle is more cruel and strict than a simple straight line and thus, through its everlasting repetition, confirms the basic clear and light *einmal ist keinmal* line of existence) did not allow Friedrich to think about this paradox that he would certainly have liked, and so the smile on his face was caused by a simpler and more easily guessed analogy, by the fact that both the wooden desk and the leaves of paper were made of the same material; only the age of this particular desk prevented the thought that the wood and the paper had been made from the same tree or maybe from two neighboring trees. Today Nietzsche was in a good and diligent frame of mind. He walked to the desk and began looking at and sorting the messy papers, attempting with a glance to read and decode a fragment of text written with his quick and hard-to-read handwriting, written when he was trying to keep up with a whole flood of his thoughts in those lucid moments when it seemed that every drop that spilled from the pot that is his head had to be absorbed by paper or it would be irretrievably lost. He succeeded in sorting a heap of individual leaves into some kind of regular mass and put it aside. Happily and contentedly he began to flip through the pages of his completed manuscripts. He touched the pages of *Ecce Homo* gently, with, it seemed, the pleasant feeling that his writings justified their own existence. He turned over the pages, reading only the subtitles, as if flipping through a newspaper. The self-conscious pathetical-vain pomposity of these subtitles elicited a happy smile. He whispered slowly the rhetorical questions that headed the chapters: *Why I am so wise, Why I am so clever, Why I write such excellent books, Why I am fate.* In those phrases there was perhaps a grain of self-irony, or at least a hint that might eventually let one detect self-irony, but still this was his opinion and this was the easiest way to express it. Someone somewhere speaking about self-praise quoted a thought of Lord Bacon—*the wisest, brightest, and meanest of mankind*—who pointed out that even for self-commendation the ancient Latin praise of slander is valuable: *Semper aliquid haeret.* Maybe Nietzsche remembered Bacon because he had noticed his name on the pages he'd flipped and subconsciously glanced at: *We hardly know enough about Lord Bacon—the first realist in the highest sense of the word—to be sure of* everything *he did,* everything *he willed, and* everything *he experienced in himself.* The other names written on the manuscript's pages must have been noticed as well: Heine, Wagner, da Vinci, Bach, Ranke, Horace. Each name brought its own associations, the same way that smell and taste evoke their own recollections and stimulate memories. He liked to think that future poets and philosophers would consider him as significant as he considered a few of his own teachers. His time was not fond of him. He put *Ecce Homo* aside and took up the manuscript of *The Antichrist,* perhaps remembering one of the first sentences in that book, a sentence he had written while thinking about himself: *Some men are born posthumously.* In fact, resentment wafted from all his works due to the absence of tribute and admiration, resentment concealed by self-love and a pose of prior knowledge and expectation or almost prophetic presentiments about the fate accorded to his writing by the times he lived in, by the fairly unenviable and rather subdued level of reception of his works. Yet, while still young, he had made *noncontemporaneity* his main goal. He was troubled most of all by the unreceptiveness of the times, but he always consoled himself with the firm belief—and on mornings like this one he believed it without a trace of suspicion—that his time would come, a time when *one day his name would be associated with the memory of something tremendous.* Already there were some sensible and prophetic souls who had not passed out from the thin mountain air of his writings. Recently he had mailed a short text about himself—an encoded life—at the request of the Danish professor Brandes. Perhaps that somewhat poetic curriculum vita had provoked him into writing *Ecce Homo,* a kind of autobiography. Brandes was not the only one who discerned his greatness. A small group of admirers scattered around the world, like some sensitive and tiny animals, apprehended the coming earthquake that would be caused by his thought, like rats they knew that the ship of contemporaneity should be abandoned, that weak and ornate yacht that has been trying for as long as possible to hide one unpleasant and uncorrectable fact—that it is sinking. He flipped through the pages and read the manuscripts till it became dark. Then he lit a lamp and sat quietly looking at the wall, probably thinking about his works in the swaying and shadowy, solemn and almost churchlike silence. Lately he could read and write under artificial light only with great difficulty. The letters were searching for the sun. He sat motionless for a long time; only his forehead would occasionally be covered with wrinkles like a sea covered with small waves stroked by a light wind. Sometimes his right hand would press his temples, covering his forehead with its span, like a kid measuring distance. When he glanced at the clock it was already nearly midnight. He lay down and, amazingly, again fell asleep quickly. His spirit sank into sleep at practically the same moment that his body sank into the bed. According to the Bible, King David always fell asleep this quickly.

1.2.1889

Nietzsche awoke at daybreak, amazed and happy. Again he had slept well and deeply. He was turning in bed, waking up. Lusciously, he rolled his tongue in satisfaction, like a dog. He was still in the thrall of yesterday's excellent mood, that almost physically tangible height of self-consciousness and agitated satisfaction. Ideas, concepts, phrases, sentences—the totality of the mental architecture and rhetorical facade of his works stood under his view, and he was satisfied with the plasticity of that phenomenon, its picturesque appearance. Along with this vision, in the background, he saw a moving sequence of the events and situations of his life from the times that certain of his works were created. He recalled certain memories and relived them in the sweet-and-sour and distressingly painless way that occurs when a self from some past period splits from the present self and they feel only a slight identification with each other as if with some imaginary personality, a figment, a personality after all not so likeable, but which has some insignificant detail that allows for identification, let's say a similarity of lips or clothing, for example. But apparently all these things he recalled so indifferently today had made his works such as they are, and so they seemed significant to him. Although his mood was closer to yesterday's than to that of two days before, his behavior was, on the contrary, closer to that of two days ago than to yesterday's. Nietzsche lay awake in bed till nearly noon, not due to some weakness this time but rather due to the satisfaction of spiritual abundance, due to the enjoyment of idleness that is (as he himself wrote before) *what a true thinker desires the most.* Still he did not intend to spend the whole day lying down. He was an ascetic in his intimate pleasures, even though in recent months he had occasionally written true praises of indulgence (actually, mostly about simple animal indulgence, indulgence in the things he himself liked). His youthful character, which to some extent was expressed in those events he had been recalling this morning, lingered more in the practical atavism of his habits than in the theoretical evolution of his writings and rhetorically formed thoughts. The similarity with yesterday's mood also repeated itself today in the will to work. As he had yesterday, Nietzsche sat at his writing desk and read his own manuscripts. But as opposed to the previous day, his inner state did not have that pleasant uniformity. In the background it was as if some undetermined shadow was waxing, a shadow that covered the sun his soul so desired, a shadow that slowly grew as after high noon. He tried to chase away or forget that unpleasant feeling by walking in the room, trying through physical activity to bring a pleasant ingredient to the dull chemistry of the complicated mechanism of his consciousness. After a while he sat again and began flipping quickly and chaotically through his manuscripts, one after another, as if searching in every one of them for a formula that would sum up his complete opus and teaching. From the background of his brain, from some sphere of the huge terra incognita that was his internal kingdom, an obsessive refrain, a chorus of unpleasant suspicion, was relentlessly emerging to the surface of his spiritual sea, and it was slowly but surely coming to occupy the front line of his mood, triumphing over yesterday's happy self-satisfaction. Most likely, the siren's song of this suspicion expressed skepticism toward the fruit of his efforts. It was something that must have been hard on him, although suspicion is in fact something *human, truly human.* It must have seemed to Nietzsche that the various casual thoughts and associations he had had over the previous two days had carried a hint as to what was now happening, like when a sailor understands the meaning of what had seemed to be an innocent cloud just before a storm breaks. Then he took up the manuscript of *The Will to Power,* a work he thought that by its name alone expressed the concrete quintessential originality and novelty of his teaching. This work, too, had been created last year. His spirit lives in all the other works from that period. *What is good?—Whatever augments the feeling of power, the will to power, power itself, in man.*—This nearly catechistical phrase, in question and answer form, is at the beginning of *The Antichrist.* But the unpleasant feeling was spreading organically through his body. Nietzsche again stood up and began walking about the room. He had no desire to go out, as if the unpleasant feeling manifested itself also in some kind of agoraphobia. Suddenly he stopped by the bedside night table, a night table with books, as if seeing it for the first time. He looked at the hardbound works of his teachers and educators. As if hypnotized, he picked up *The World as Will and Representation.* Then perhaps he remembered Dostoyevsky, *the only psychologist from whom he learned anything, a psychologist who belongs to the most beautiful happy moments of his life.* In one Dostoyevsky novel, a German (apropos—Dostoyevsky, *that* deep *man, was right ten times over to devalue trivial Germans*) looks for answers to his dilemmas by opening the Bible at random and taking the first sentence he sees as a prophecy, as a kind of Pythian perfect advice to be followed. At random Friedrich opened the Bible of his youth: *The World as Will and Representation.* The heavy tome opened to the beginning of the fifty-fourth chapter. Nietzsche's glance fell on the next-to-last sentence of the second paragraph: *Since the will always wants life, exactly because life is nothing else but a manifestation of that will in representation, it is completely unimportant, it is just a pleonasm, if instead of saying simply* will *we say* will to live. Nietzsche read this sentence aloud several times, and then closed and put aside the book. He sat on the bed and stared at the wall. He must have been remembering two opposite pages of his experience that stood for the two poles of his youth: his education of a philologist and his enthusiasm for Schopenhauer. Now these two poles melted together in some kind of metaphysical disappointment. Perhaps it seemed to him that his whole life was just a pleonasm. Because what is the will for power other than the most ordinary will to live or simply just will, the blind will of Schopenhauer. He had dedicated his life to a phantom. And perhaps he remembered his pure youthful love for Schopenhauer, a love he had betrayed so nastily so many times in last year's writings, like a divorced husband slandering the former wife whom he still loves above all. He was disgusted by this yearning for his youth, just as he was disgusted by all vulgar commonplaces, but he was also yearning for sincerity, for a source, for health, strength, vigor, enthusiasm. Outside it was getting darker, as it was in his soul. Nietzsche probably sat in the dark till after midnight.

1.3.1889

Opening his eyes this morning, Nietzsche did not know if he had awakened. In fact, he was not sure if he slept at all last night. He had spent the whole night in some giddy delirium, a surrogate of sleep. It was overcast outside. The first clouds of the new year were floating above Turin. Immediately after opening his eyes, which could be called awakening only by inertia, Nietzsche got dressed and went out. He had not left the house for a full two days. He went out into the fresh air driven perhaps by some ancient instinct, some almost archetypical hope that relief would come from fresh air in open spaces. It was still early and the streets were deserted. The first sign of life he saw was a carriage on the corner. He heard a whistle, but not a whistle made by the wind. As Friedrich approached the corner with the carriage, the whistle became mixed with the sound of his footsteps and the coachman's cruel cursing. The incisive scream of a whip nearly covered the horse's painful groan. At the street corner, the laughing coachman was beating the horse with a thick leather whip, beating it cruelly, bloodily, and for no reason. With his eyes frothing, the coachman watched a neat and refined gentleman approach him. He began hitting the horse even harder, more briskly and more frequently. The thick bristly mustache of the slowly approaching gentleman was visibly trembling. The coachman thought that Nietzsche was laughing approvingly. But in fact Nietzsche was looking into the horse's sad eyes, into the animal's terribly sad eyes. His already slow steps became shaky and insecure as a drunkard's. With his last remaining strength he came up to the horse and embraced it firmly, running his hands through its mane like a man playing with the hair of his beloved. His shoulders were heaving in an almost fatal spasm. The whip in coachman's hand froze and became mute. Perhaps for a moment the coachman thought that he was dreaming. The gentlemanly pedestrian embraced the horse and shed tears. For the first time since his childhood Friedrich Nietzsche was crying.

Translated from the Bosnian by Oleg Andrić and Andrew Wachtel

■ □ ■ □ ■

THE POET

But delusions follow poets,
Don't you know that they loiter about in every valley,
And preach what they do not do,

Koran 36:224–26

Dear Editor,
I am addressing you because among the public servants of words I regard you to be, at the moment, the best interpreter and specialist regarding the person and opus of Muhamed Dženetić. The most recent issue of your *Literary Almanac,* completely dedicated to the friend whom I have never stopped mourning, cheered me and gave me great pleasure, first of all because of the elementary intellectual and artistic respect signified by observing and judging his opus from a literary standpoint, and not, as is the custom today, from the standpoint of a comparison between his work and his life. Some points from your introduction, like the one that *all of today's poets are just miscarried and aborted children of Dženetić,* I myself—of course somewhat differently formulated and without the penetration and vehemence of your authorial style—have expounded in private conversations on more than one occasion. But what prodded me to write this letter is not the majority of your various views, so diametrically different from the notions published by the whole pack of journalists, critics, and other scribblers on the fifteenth anniversary of his death. I am writing to you—exactly for the opposite reason—because of the (maybe the only) part of your introduction where your opinion to some extent adheres to the commonplaces of the local critical judgment of my friend's grandiose work. I am

writing—let me remind you—apropos of the paragraph where you state:

In the world of art the conflict between life and work is a matter of course. Baudelaire is a poser par excellence. Decadents on paper from the romantic period achieved orgasm merely by holding the naked foot of their beloved. Unhappy Wilde created works as wavy as a silk scarf, while contented and balanced Chesterton wrote down his nightmares. Schopenhauer, at a groaning board, preached voluntary starvation. Nietzsche, the prophet of cruelty, was gentle as a virgin. It is true that this same Nietzsche had written that a philosopher worthy of respect had to preach by example, but Socrates and his Danish reincarnation who held to this were just exceptions that confirmed the rule. It is stupid and senseless, therefore, to attack the amazingly admirable work of Muhamed Dženetić with objections because, perhaps, it does not match his life. Etc., etc.

It is clear to me that even here you—to put it banally—are on my friend's side and that you are defending him, but things are not so simple. This is why I—convinced of your good intentions—will in this letter reveal some facts—until now known only to me—that will necessarily be intertwined with certain well-known facts. For the work of my friend does have its key in his life, though this key is not obvious and banal but masked by various ephemeral things and his conscious camouflage, in the same way that sometimes in his poems—in the manner of symbolism—he hides simple words and meanings behind magical metaphors and allegories. Muhamed Dženetić was born, as you know, on January 8, 1918, in Sarajevo. For very many years his family had been—as it is said—ulemas.[1] His father was a kadi[2] (and also a hafiz),[3] two of his uncles were imams,[4] and among his ancestors were several well-known alims.[5] I believe you can imagine the atmosphere in which Muhamed spent his childhood, the worldview breathed by his natal house, and the upbringing he was given without me overburdening you with commonplace folkloric details and anecdotes. In fact, what I know about this is derived from his stories, so I could actually only be a secondhand source. In that period I did not know him. Our acquaintance began when we both attended the Sharia[6] high school in Sarajevo, and it is from that time on that I can talk about my personal impressions of my friend. In the special supplement to the most recent issue of your magazine *Photos from the Family Album of Muhamed Dženetić,* you published a photo of our class at the end of our senior year of high school. The face of my friend is circled by marker, and that thick irregular circle covers the heads of the people on his left and right. Well, the person on the left—that is me. It was in fact some time during that year that our more intensive friendship began. I have often heard stories claiming that, as a rule, we do not remember the concrete event that brings a true friend into our life, but I—as if to spite them—do remember. You should know that the Sharia High School was not a classic religious school, not a madrasah.[7] It was a public school with all of the subjects of "ordinary" high schools plus additional Sharia classes. This means that we studied—in addition to Arabic—Latin, French, and German, studied—as well—mathematics, physics, and chemistry and of course our mother tongue and its literature—Serbian at the time. But, still, the majority of the students had already mapped out in their heads the future profession of imam, and they treated "Vlach"[8] subjects with contempt. My father, however, was a freethinking man—today he would be called a liberal—so in that period I already saw my future in a secular college. That is why I, not so much through my own will as due to the circumstances, excelled in these "non-Sharia" classes. And although I was only fourteen or fifteen years old, I was a well-read boy since my father had a rich library crowded with books from—as it is said—all walks of life. So, after a literature class during which a teacher talked about Dostoyevsky and I succeeded in getting praised for mentioning the titles of a few of his books—which I had not read, by the way, I had known the titles only from the spines—I was approached by Muhamed, who asked me if I could give him a book by Dostoyevsky to read. I said I had to ask my father and invited him to go home with me so that I could give him a book immediately if my father agreed. While we walked toward my house he asked me questions (mostly about Dostoyevsky), while I answered tersely and vaguely, as people do when they do not know each other well but happen to be alone. Of course my father agreed to let me lend a book to my friend, and I immediately gave him one—I believe it was *The Insulted and Injured.* That same day I began reading *The Brothers Karamazov.* That was perhaps the most fateful day in my life: I found a friend and discovered atheism. Maybe it is better to say that I discovered the possibility of atheism, but nonetheless from that day on things were no longer simple. The world had become a riddle. Muhamed returned the book the next day, and I gave him another one, but it is important that from that day on our friendship grew deeper and stronger. Now we had something in common to talk about. I well remember our walks deep in thought, when we would sometimes be startled by the sound of a streetcar bell and then we would jump out of the way at the last moment. I remember a bench by the Evangelical church where we used to sit and converse (later on we learned to smoke there). I remember attending jumuah[9] and teraweeh[10] together, as well as the first coffee we drank once just after a jumuah. I remember our rare soccer matches on the high school field and our school picnics on Trebević. I remember our first mature conversations, too (I always started them): about girls and the political situation. I remember we started buying *Politika*—one day it was him, the next day me—and we read it together—I read the articles about politics and acted concerned, he read serial novels and the comics (I remember Mickey Mouse and Secret Agent X-9). But I have gotten ahead of myself. I forgot for a moment that after Dostoyevsky I lent him other books almost every day—mostly poetry. While Dostoyevsky led me to philosophy, he helped him to discover poetry. I remember—and you probably know this—that his first poet—the first poet whom he admired—was Pushkin. I often think of how ironic it is that the public view of my friend as a poet is almost a carbon copy of his view of the poets he loved. He could not have separated Pushkin's poems from his interest in our folk poetry, from his death in a duel, and finally from his predecessor—grandfather or great-grandfather—Ibrahim (you certainly know that Pushkin's direct predecessor was an African boy, Ibrahim, who was bought at the Istanbul slave market by our countryman and given as a gift to Czar Peter the Great). And my friend's first poem was dedicated precisely to Pushkin. He burned it as he burned almost all his "schoolboy" poems (the few that were saved were published—as you know only posthumously) although it would have fit perfectly into his celebrated cycle "To the Ancestors of My Dreams." Even today I remember that in that poem he mentioned Dante and d'Anthès on the basis of contrast and alliteration. From his first poem until his student days my friend read passionately, wrote and mostly destroyed his poems. As far as reading goes, Pushkin was followed by other Russians, and afterward by French, Germans, English. As you know he was never fond of our poets. In this period there occurred what somewhere you called *the paradigmatic dusk—the situation in which the sun—whether we like it or not—goes West and we have to follow.* That dusk—as you could already have guessed—occurred one generation earlier in my family (my father followed that sun), while in the Dženetić family the first *flirtation with the other* was performed by Muhamed. His family saw him at Al-Ashar (where his elder brother had already been a brilliant student for three years) when he (with two more years of high school still in front of him) announced to them that he would prefer to study something secular in Belgrade. I know of the web of shock and excitement that followed only from Muhamed, and therefore I do not want to burden you by retelling the story. In the end, against his wishes, his father finally agreed, consoled perhaps by his firstborn and conscious of the folk saying that it is better to give in to a younger son if he is already a black sheep. That is how, in 1936, Muhamed enrolled in the fourteenth group of sciences (Serbian language and literature) in Belgrade, and I enrolled in law school. For four years we were roommates in the Gajret student dorm on Dalmatia Street. You know that his first collection of poems was published in 1939 and that it contains mostly poems from the period between 1936 and 1938. Are you interested in knowing how they were created? Whenever I was startled by a noise an hour or two after we had gone to sleep, I knew he had gotten up to write. He told me that he would see a flash of a word or a combination of words in the darkness while trying to fall asleep—a metaphor, a comparison or allegory—and then around it, as around a grain of sand in a pearl-oyster shell, a poem would be created and twined. Exactly this comparison is that grain of sand in the Shakespearian sonnet "Ars Poetica." (You surely remember the final couplet:

The words hurt me, creating maladies
As a stone when it tears the inside of a shell.)

What do you think the first "Belgrade" poem was? It was the rubai[11] "The Estuary." He wrote it long ago during one of those first

September nights of our first Belgrade year. Even had I not heard or read it again, I believe I would still know it by heart today:

You flow by hills, lakes, roads,
You flow through mountains and yellow fields.
Like a vein through a body you pass through the earth
To be swallowed by death from the Black Forest.

You know yourself how frequently—especially earlier—the prophetic dimension of this poem was accentuated and emphasized. And you surely remember the witch hunt in the midseventies targeted at my friend when, apropos of a selection of his poetry in German translation, in conversation for *Literatur Zeitung,* he made the statement that Hitler—if nothing else—gave him the opportunity to discover Nietzsche. (Muhamed read Nietzsche—you know that anyway—for the first time during World War II when he bought his collected works in some German bookstore in Sarajevo.) The poem "To Zarathustra" with its clear emphatic beginning opens the cycle "To the Ancestors of My Dreams." Do you remember these verses—today especially timely?

You give me back faith, brother,
That the Balkans are not just a slaughterhouse,
But when are they finally going to understand
That the universe was interpreted here.
Because would there be art at all
If here sometime long ago
The Birth of Tragedy had not occurred
In unique Hellenic light?

Do you remember *reflections and reactions* regarding *a reputed prophet who warned about Nazi aggression and was now thanking Hitler,* how Dženetić *for the nth time has put his foot into his own mouth, etc., etc.*? Apropos of the cycle "To the Ancestors of My Dreams," it seems to me that your favorite poem from that string of unusual thank-you poems is that gorgeous dedication *to the first among the decadent* under the title "Heautontimoroumenos":

He changed the direction of poetry
He seated Satan's clergy

He was a sparrow that facit ver
A sufferer for the muse—Charles Baudelaire.

You wrote somewhere that *in this poem Dženetić, like a craftsman, draws a perfect portrait in four strokes.* But in those four strokes there are—as you say—*an allusion to Baudelaire's view of the modern intellectual as the heir of the clergy, and a hint of his closeness to the Latin language (in addition to titling numerous poems in* The Flowers of Evil *in Latin, the poet even wrote one whole poem in Latin), and many more.* But I was talking—I believe—about our student life. Those were beautiful days. The first fall and winter the two of us spent in our room, cocooned like larvae in hibernation. In the mornings we went to lectures, coming back in the early afternoons—sometimes he found me already in the room, sometimes I found him—and the rest of the day we spent keeping quiet, or in empty conversation and in that freshman drawl that must have looked like studying. On Saturdays and Sundays, our whole day was like that. We would go out once a week—not counting trips to the university and the cafeteria—mostly to get some fresh air. I remember one of those evening walks—if it is not the quintessence or archetype of all of our walks fused into one by my memory. Pressed one next to the other and hunched over, looking at the attractive posters and bar entrances, we felt—for the first time—our own insignificance, minuteness, and negligibility in the huge mass of unknown people, as well as the noise, speed, and heavy breathing of urban turbulence and the crowd that are—in the well-known words of my friend—*the main characteristics of our age.* You can already suppose that after one such a walk the famous elegy "How to Feel My Own Existence" with these oft-quoted verses was created:

I am a fraction whose numerator grows with every passing moment
While under pressure the denominator becomes more and more a
shadow.

Not only this but almost all of the poems from this period were created after such walks. Among the most well known is certainly the miniature "The Preacher"—which you call *a quatrain that fuses an Old Testament lament, pagan Roman wisdom, and a fascinating and completely new modern metaphor.* Even today when I read all those stupidities about my friend I console myself with these words of his:

Nothing new under the sun
Always bread and circuses
Only stupidity gets thicker
Like a pudding as it cooks.

But I conveyed the wrong impression to you if you think that this period was depressing for us and that the walks of these unadulterated provincials—as my friend would have said—were an unpleasant experience. Quite the contrary, it was in this period that the rubai "The Harmony of the World"—your favorite poem of my friend's, I would say—was created. I write it here for your delectation:

I light a cigarette and a blackbird is already whistling.
I inhale the smoke—My pride returns.
The smoke is the paintbrush of a great artist
Who makes cosmos out of chaos.

You too—as well as myself—will be reminded of your youth. Your famous essay "The Apotheosis of Tobacco"—the first you wrote about my friend, while he was still alive—is about this poem. You were—I think—still a student (as, in fact, was my friend when he wrote this poem—the inspiration for your essay) when in using this example you revealed all the stupidity of our criticism. You wrote:

. . . And so—according to our criticism—this poem is merely a rubai in form without any sense and internal charge. It would have been more intelligent for the old word-eaters and ruminants to remain silent as stones in the face of this young genius of only twenty. And, did forty years have to pass, wasn't there anyone before me with the elementary literacy to stop this spiteful mockery of the celebrated "academic bard"—to whom someone should finally say barba non facit philosopher—*who "does not need a cigarette to turn a truck into a lorry."* O sancta simplicitas! *Oh holy stupidity! Doesn't anyone here know the fundamentals of ancient Greek? Doesn't anyone know that in Greek the word* kosmos, *in addition to meaning the world and the universe, also means order? And naive Dženetić even used an accent*

sign to tell the reader that this is a foreign word so as to make it easier to understand. But he really overestimates the society to which he directs the book. Does anyone even now understand the magic of this poem? Does he find, at least in his own experience, that moment when, by lighting a cigarette, chaos turns into harmony? . . . Don't even let me get started talking about how he translates the exact spirit of a rubai, its melody and flow of thought, into our language. I will just note that I don't know whether anyone before Dženetić so glorified tobacco in poetry. If Jose Ortega y Gasset is right when he says there are two basic types of people—the first are happy when they are "out of control" and the second are happy when they are "in control"—and that these two types differ from each other in all spheres of life, then Dženetić is perhaps the first humanlike poet *(as Ambrose Bierce would have said) who celebrates being in control in such a grandiose way. Because coffee and cigarettes are* drugs of in-control *unlike alcohol, which has already been adored in poetry so many times. The Russians: Mayakovsky and Mandelstam did it most beautifully.*

It is better
to die from vodka
than from boredom!

Or

I will tell you with the utmost
Candor:
All is folly—sherry-brandy—
Angel mine . . .

But unlike these Russian poets, so near and dear to him, Dženetić does not glorify alcohol, but tobacco. Etc., etc. . . .

Truly, we smoked like crazy then. My friend, in his last book, as you know, would talk about tobacco again, this time using the Western, baroque, sonnet form:

ONTOLOGICAL HYPOTHESIS

While a man lies in darkness and smokes
Strange thoughts go through his mind.
The normal order of things collapses
Breaking like vases, ceramic and brittle.

The cigarette glows when smoke is inhaled.
The room, in an instant, is light as dawn.
But immediately darkness returns
Until the next breath that looks like a noose.

Maybe the sun is in fact a smoldering cigarette,
The day is then a gift from a breath of smoke,
While night is just a pause for exhalation.

Wars, floods, or droughts—all is vanity
Summer, fall, winter—a tiny human memory,
The whole history of the planet—one cigarette.

But one of those first walks seemed as if it was a prophecy of that Belgrade we would get accustomed to and fall in love with. On that October walk on Terazije, on the spot where Knez Mihajlova and Kolarčeva Streets reach the square, we found a crowd of people gathered in and around some dive. We mingled with the crowd. There was singing and crying. We did not have time to light a cigarette before we were each handed a drink. We arrived just as fall's dusk was turning into evening, we stayed until after midnight. For the two of us, it was the first touch of what is modishly called *nightlife* today. You are wondering: what kind of a party was this? It was a kind of a requiem for the famous dive Albania. You probably know that on the site of today's palace called Albania—that symbol of modern Belgrade—there used to be a bar with the same name. That night the demolition of the bar had been announced, and Belgraders were saying good-bye in this way to their cherished meeting place. We were there among those sad and joyful people and we sipped our drinks—truth be told, I drank rather than sipped—until sometime around midnight when a group of workers with sledgehammers showed up. (*Sledgehammers spoiled our sipping—a beautiful alliteration at least*—my friend said.) Together with the mass we moved away and then, protesting, we watched the ramshackle walls being smashed. My friend was the first—and many followed him—to take a piece of the wall. To his biographers this is an unknown detail and it was only in 1989—when the pieces of another wall became a relic—that I even recalled his truly prophetic spirit. This whole evening left a strong impression on

Muhamed, and it was—this is also unknown to the public—the inspiration for the well-known poem "The Life of Things" with its epigraph from Daudet (where he mentions nightlife in his own way): *Mais la nuit, c'est la vie des choses.* The verses

> *The lives of people are bad dreams,*
> *Just burblings of deception and magic.*
> *In vain a man longs for reality*
> *In fact only things are real.*

were inspired exactly by the little bar Albania where—in fact—we spent only one evening. But you should know that we compared the flow of our student days precisely with the growth of the titanic building that was rising on the site of our first Belgrade bar. Because it took three years to build this famous palace. It was completed just around the time of the publication of my friend's first book. But by then we were—as Muhamed was wont to say—*old Belgraders.* We were—among other things—evening habitués of bars, frequent users of the services of the National Library, somewhat less frequent attendees at the National Theater and the Kolarčev People's University, and true city rats who knew all the steep cobbled peripheral streets (not to mention the city center), embankments and levees, parks with young couples, passages and shortcuts, all the corners and holes-in-the-wall of Kalemegdan from King Street and Zindan Gate to Jakšić Street and Dizdarov Tower. Even now almost every evening, I recall Belgrade's half twilight when street lamps are being lit, streetcars are getting crowded, and young men and women are hurrying to their rendezvous. This is when the air is suddenly permeated with smells, as if the nose is taking its revenge on the eye for its daily supremacy. And a few months after the publication of my friend's famous firstborn *The Hum of a Shell at Night,* more precisely on December 27, 1939—as you know, a poem with this date in its title would open his second book (i.e., *The Second Book*)—he first met his only love and his future wife Eleonora nee Zorić. A lot has been written about this love, a lot of guesses have been made (you know yourself that my friend spoke about his own deepest essence only through his poems). I was a witness to the creation of this love (in the true sense of creation because it was not that it was born and grew but rather it was created, as it were, ex nihilo). It occurred at a dance in the building of the Agricultural Cooperative Union on Poincaré Street. That is the motivation for the *mysterious poem dedicated to Poincaré*—as you called it. Because it wasn't clear to anyone what a politician was doing in the poetry of a poet who had always despised politics. And although I like your theory about that poem (you called *a poetic speculation*)—in which you say that the poem *about Poincaré is . . . an ode to growing up with newspapers—that first symptom of* a global village. *Because throughout his life Dženetić bought* Politika *in remembrance of his youth. And today's Macedonia Street—where the* Politika *building is situated, used to be called Poincaré Street*—I have to tell you that you are wrong. But still you are half right. You discovered that the key is in the name of the street, and not in the person after whom the street was named (had the person been relevant, then this poem could probably be read as Muhamed's homage to Mayakovsky, who mentions Poincaré in his poem "Kiev"). You even guessed that my friend dedicated a poem to growing up with newspapers, but that is a completely different poem—the one with an epigraph from Camus: *From time to time I imagine what future historians will say about us. One sentence will be enough though to describe modern man: he was debauched and read newspapers,* where Muhamed says:

I am just half modern
Like a centaur who is just half a horse.
The smell of printing ink is less strange to me
Than the stink of sweat or sperm.

But I was talking about that famous date. The two of us arrived at the dance pretty late. Some couples were already leaving. She was sitting in a chair in the corner, in a rather large mixed company. That well-known photography of Muhamed and Eleonora printed in *The Photos from a Family Album* shows her already in middle age, but even there her beauty is stunning. You cannot even imagine how she looked that evening. Our era—along with other victims—killed elegancy, too (Muhamed used to say that elegancy by way of alliteration practically adheres to her name). Today when I remember that night at the last breath of 1939 and the thirties in general, I am gripped by nostalgia. I almost have Goethe's feeling (in light of that sentence of his, so dear to Muhamed, *My space, that is time*). Because I yearn for lost time, and nostalgia is—originally—a grief for lost space—homesickness. But who knows, had I not already been crazy over *Politika* and politics, perhaps I would myself have approached *the siren in the black dress*—as my friend, whispering in my ear, called the unknown beauty as soon as he saw her. He would repeat that formulation—remember?—in the poem "To Homer (Or Ulysses)." He—the exemplar of shyness—asked her to dance and, as in a dream, as they began to talk about literature she mentioned the fabulous poems of some young man—some Muhamed Dženetić. Everything was decided by the end of that night. She was studying French, and was—like him—a college senior and exactly ten months younger—born on November 8, 1918. To keep it short, they both graduated in September of the following year, in October they got married, and in November Muhamed took her to his home in Sarajevo. Here our paths split for some time. I remained in Belgrade, less because of school (I had two exams left), but more because of the Party.[12] I don't see any need to write to you about myself (you can already guess that I don't want you to publish this letter even under that worn-out journalistic formula *name and address known to the editors*), but I must at least en passant mention the reasons why I am unable to speak about my friend's life in the following few years from the position of an eyewitness. I was recruited by the Party sometime during my sophomore year of college and at first I tried to engage Muhamed although I could certainly have guessed that he would not show any interest. His indifference did not derive from—as my Party friends would have said—the higher level of conservativeness in his family. It was simply a matter of his character and nature. Although I tried *to stake* on his poetic feeling of justice and talked to him about the Party more in lyrical pictures than in commissariat phrases, his response was an undeveloped paraphrase of his much later publicistic statement:

The choice between poetry and politics for me has never been difficult one. (Here I am not thinking about that so-called following politics that manifests itself in bar babble and in the reading of newspapers.) I have always felt like a tourist in this world, and if I were, as a tourist in some picturesque area offered glasses or binoculars by a guide, I would always pick the binoculars. I would like to say that where politics looks two meters ahead, poetry looks miles ahead. If I have ever had ambitions, my only ambition has been—as Franz Liszt said—to throw a spear into the future.

So on December 27, 1939—in other words on that night when my friend discovered the love of his life—Poland, rather than any girl, was in my thoughts. As you know the only—albeit cursory—mention of war in my friend's second book (which was created in the period between 1939 to 1945) is that poem with an epigraph from Baudelaire: *Je suis le soufflet et la joue,* in which my friend says:

A victim and a torturer are one and the same
two layers of silk of maya.
Better to be hunted than the hunter
Though the essence be a hundred times the same.

Somewhere you wrote beautifully:

And although Dženetić himself says that for him, seemingly paradoxically, "only Schopenhauer's completely irrational philosophy explains the world in a way worthy of mind, ratio," *he still in this poem goes counter to his own philosophical and metaphysical view in favor of ethics, in favor of the famous Talmudic view that places—as does Spinoza—ethics above all other manifestations of the* worldly spirit.

And I, though I graduated in February of 1941, still remained in Belgrade. At the end of March I was in the crowd that yelled *bolje rat nego pakt*[13] (my friend would later tell me that it was a true miracle that anything good happened from such a bad and coarse assonant rhyme), on April 6 I survived the bombardment. Although my war experience coincided for the most part with the chronology of offensives that you studied in elementary school (which today, in any case, is not something to brag about), still I managed to meet with Muhamed even during the war. It was in early spring of 1942. I was in Sarajevo on a mission—as they say—and I could not resist going to his house one evening at dusk. I am writing this to you primarily to explain that *strange and mysterious poem where emotion somewhat masks Dženetić's strongly expressed need for perfection*—as you wrote somewhere. It was precisely this visit of mine that was the motivation for the verses

After eighteen months
Like after two pregnancies
Those seven years again
Are not empty years of loneliness.

I am amazed by the fact that in Nietzsche—whom Muhamed read at the time—you also found a comparison with a pregnancy of eighteen months. I even remember that I saw *Ecce Homo* on Muhamed's desk during this visit. That, even to me who knew Muhamed so well and to whom this poem, ultimately, was dedicated, revealed some secrets of his poetic mechanism, the enormity of his genius that could always find the root of his emotion. Because eighteen months had truly passed, and without these *two pregnancies* a poem could not have been created. I spent that evening reading his new poems. I was no longer his first reader—Eleonora had taken my place. And although the first war year—with Užice, Foča, and Igman—had pretty well battered my previously gentle youthful nature and although at first sight I did not like the fact that the verses so obviously lacked any war reflections, I was soon touched anew with the full magic of my friend's poetical genius. Among these poems was that one you like so much, the sonnet "Indian Summer." It reminded me immediately of our difficult first Belgrade days when both eyes and thoughts were winging southward. Even now, every year when September passes into October I remember those words:

Mugginess heavy, stiff
Thoughts crumbling like a wedge
Leaden silence floats
Air is redolent of spleen.

Anomie, sleepiness, exhaustion.
Apathy spreads.
Boredom, restlessness, gloom,
The smell of flowering roses.

Ascetic fervor,
Spring pilgrimage,
Tramp of faraway steps,

Contours of fall, melancholy,
Bells, inverse of summer,
Wax, hourglass.

You return to this sonnet (as you have so many times before) in the introduction to your magazine's most recent issue:

And what else can be said about the sonnet "Indian Summer"? In fourteen lines with the help of forty-one words (even this numerical palindrome is not accidental) we find an ideal model, the crux of that basic emotion that has persecuted poets forever and especially from Poe until today. This is the unattainable ideal of the entire Matoš-Dučić l'art pour l'art *school in our poetry. And, as in a painting, this poem joins pre-Renaissance strictness, the formal harmony of the Renaissance itself, and a baroque warning memento mori, while the whole is bridged, as by an arch, by a basic Stimmung of romantic symbolism—by the Dürer-like melancholy of a bored God and by the resignation of a fallen angel.*

I saw here almost all of the poems he would publish under the title *Other Things* in his second book. The other poems from that collection—those from the cycle "To the Ancestors of My Dreams" and from that seven-piece cycle with an epigraph from Kierkegaard: *The pureness of heart is in wishing one and only one thing*—I would read only after the war. You know yourself that there were even "self-proclaimed critics" who did not understand that each of those seven poems—"Eleonora (Or 12/27/1939)," "Ela," "Leonora," "Lena," "Lenka," "Nora," and "Lea"—were dedicated to the same woman—the only one whom he loved and wrote poems to—his wife, and they spoke about his "ironic epigraph." *Oh holy stupidity*—as you have already said. By the way, let me say he really used all these names for his wife (and many others). In various periods of their lives, various names "ruled." But—be that as it may—I had to leave the next day after breakfast. The war led me from the Neretva to Srijem. At Sutjeska I was wounded and was taken care of by a certain nurse from Dalmatia whom I would later marry. I was married in Belgrade—like my friend—in the late spring of 1945, the early spring of freedom. A month after the wedding I went to Sarajevo to visit my family and Muhamed. Everything was all right except that Muhamed's brother, in that postwar chaos, ended up in jail by mistake. I freed him with the help of some of my connections. My friend's second book was completed. He—as you know—did not publish at all during the occupation. His family—like mine, for the most part—had lived quietly and aloof on all those stockpiles that are regularly found in well-off homes. One night I read his poems. We both knew that they did not fit into the trend of *renewal and rebuilding.* At that time I stayed in Sarajevo for a month, then my wife and I returned to Belgrade, and in the fall we moved to Zagreb (I was given a job and an apartment there). As you have probably noticed by the stamp and postmark, I still live here today. My friend's second collection with the simple title *The Second Book* and with the subtitle *About a Woman, Poets, and Other Things* was published—as you know—in 1949. In that period—between 1945 and 1949—we saw each other pretty rarely and for short periods. You know how that goes—I was building a home, had a son, and there was a lot of work. But in summer of the following year a particular kind of ritual began, which lasted about twenty years—our vacations together. That year my friend got a job—and his wife too—it was thanks to me, in part. As you know, he began to work on the editorial board of the magazine *Echo.* More tranquil days began—in Muhamed's words:

All has to be slow,
Now tumult irritates,
Now the fruits of life ripen
In the peace of midday.

You know better than I that it is precisely in the fifties and sixties that Muhamed becomes a famous poet. No doubt you know all those anecdotes told about him in Sarajevo by heart. But he remains true to himself—you know that he never published even a single one of his poems in *Echo,* in fact, nothing but some translations. He could see his poems only in books. And it was precisely in this period that his third and most voluminous book *The Diary* was created. (The book would—as you know—be published in 1969 and you wrote about it—with your usual inspiration—under the title "The Poetry of the Everyday.") Of these twenty years we spent at least two together (a month each year at the seaside in addition to other pleasant and unpleasant causes—holidays, family births and deaths, birthdays). But—I flatter myself—more than a tenth of poems in *The Diary*—maybe even a fifth—were written during our vacations. In the first years those were vacations in hotels in Opatija or Poreč, but, in the midfifties, my wife and I built a house in her hometown near Zadar. From then on we always vacationed there in the summertime. The content of those vacations can be beautifully recognized in the context of *The Diary*. There are "A Poem about a Seagull," "Moon and High Tide," "A Breakfast on the Sand," "Sea Sunrise," etc., etc. There is of course that famous poem, that—as you say—*fantastic postmodern sonnet "Je-Lena."* At first sight it is not clear where it was created, but I remember Muhamed reading it to me on a late August morning as the fruit of the previous night's labor. Yes, I heard these verses from poet's lips just after they were created:

JE-LENA

More beautiful than the one born of foam
Because of her the Cyclops's pupil darkened
And Ulysses went through Hades as a shadow
The destruction of Troy was her price

For Andrić Vienna was lonely without her
Gnostic Sophia is her counterpart
Transient as the moon's phases
Permanent as Apollo, Poseidon, Selena

Her sleepy figure mesmerized Poe
Because it is easy for her to get to her booty
Standing still like a lazy spider
She is Goethe's eternal feminine

They call her Jelena or Helena
Jelena is my Lena, is Lena.

I remember too how in July 1968 the poem "What Shall We Do?" was created, that—as you put it—*epigrammatic summary of ultimate questions,* the final one of the poems in Muhamed's third collection because—I'll reveal a secret to you—in *The Diary* as in a real diary the poems are organized simply by the chronology of their creation. Even today I often repeat this poem to myself, the best sketch of the basic human dilemma, a dilemma without an answer:

Raise barricades or
Tend one's garden?
Search for a better life or
Prepare for death?

(You said it beautifully: *a mundane political phrase, a quote from Voltaire, another phrase, a quote from Socrates, Kierkegaard's rhyme, Matoš's rhyme = Dženetić's poem.)*

The essence of our vacations is in these poems. I cannot go into details here. It is difficult to talk openly about personal, deeply intimate things. There are, though, two ways—be poetically fuzzy like my friend, or remain silent as I do. But I must mention a few phrases that my friend would repeat almost like a refrain in our long nocturnal conversations after our wives and my children (he did not have any) went to sleep: *Only here with you can I relax. I can be what I am. I think only here with you and alone with Ela. In Sarajevo I playact with everyone. I pretend I am someone else. I do not want to, but I must.* And it really was like that. You know the kind of misapprehension that existed about my friend as a living sponge. It is true—let it be clear—that he liked to drink alcohol—mostly wine and homemade herbal brandy—but always in comparatively small amounts. Three or four shots of hard liquor or half a liter of wine were his nightly dose. He said it, in any case, in that rubai published in the small epilogue to *The Diary*—"To the Ancestors of My Dreams." He writes:

A collection of poetry, half a liter of wine,
A crust of dried bread—mute silence,
And I and you alone around us a desert
That is a kingdom and not a crown made of rubies.

Where Khayyam says *a small barrel,* my friend says *half a liter.* And you yourself wrote:

But the epilogue to The Diary, *the cycle "To the Ancestors of My Dreams," is a special gem. On the one hand a subtle link with his previous collection, and on the other the first breath of the postmodern in our poetry. In this way it is avant-garde even for world literature. Dženetić again writes the poems of* the ancestors of his dreams *after having dreamed them according to his own vision and logic.*

And those stories about my friend as a great Don Juan. Listen, if there has ever been a man who loved his wife and if there has ever been a man for whom the *singular* (in every sense) was the *conditio sine qua non* of love, then it was my friend. He admitted to me that the well-known poem "Either-Or" was created after some reputed friend of his reproached him for having too much confidence in his wife. That poem expresses the essence of Muhamed's and of every other true love:

When you love someone you must trust him.
Otherwise what is the sense?
Because either souls melt together
Or you love so as to breathe faster.

For that, it seems, we do not need examples from his poetry—it is all in that spirit. That he flirted—of course. But these were—as his beloved Kierkegaard would have said—long-distance flirts in which the only weapon is the eye. And he never initiated even these, he would just sometimes—perhaps jokingly—respond with a significant look. Often even his wife's presence he spoke about stolen smiles—insinuations of promises, and she laughed together with us.

But in the year that *The Diary* was published the idyll of his themes came to an end. That winter Eleonora got sick. During the three years of her illness my friend did not—as you know—write a single verse. Everything that he did had a single purpose—to help her. That three-year-long metamorphosis from a talkative contemplative man into a man of instant action would have its later echo in the poem whose epigraph is again taken from Baudelaire: *In the world where action is not the sister of dream* and where it bitterly says:

In torment, at the end and at the beginning
Words are needless, vain,
Because in key moments
Only work, sighs, and tears count.

In 1972 Eleonora died and just then foreign publishers and translators began contacting my friend. Maybe it was precisely my friend's complete confusion and apathy at the time that encouraged his international success. He signed contracts automatically without any conditions (in any other circumstances he would surely have been a bit careful), and in the following two years nine collections of his poetry were published in (for the most part) important languages. But despite all this, my friend did not recover until 1976. Then—in fact—he discovered Poe and Venice. Accidentally, he reread "The Raven" and—as sometimes happens in literature—the similarity of events consoled him somewhat. Shortly afterward he went to Venice for a promotion of an Italian edition of his poetry. He was almost sixty years old when he found the place of his dreams. You know that in 1980 this gave birth to—in your words *the most modern and the most eternal (is it necessary also to say the best) book of our poetry—The Raven in Venice.* Here for the first time my friend writes a long poem—the title poem. You described and interpreted it like this:

This poem is perfection. Here Dženetić made the most out of the impossible. *He created a poem about love and death that corresponds to one worldly and one local masterpiece, being the first to see their similarity in form and content (how could we have been so blind?) and he created the final part of what would be from now on an immortal triptych. "The Raven" and love for the dead Lenora; "Santa Maria Della Salute" and love for the dead Lenka;* The Raven in Venice *and love for the dead Eleonora. Edgar Allan Poe; Laza Kostić; Muhamed Dženetić. The name of Dženetić's beloved unites the names of Poe's and Kostić's darlings, just like Dženetić's poem melds the poems of these two into one. In some twenty-six sestinas with a final emphatic refrain—Dženetić unites the* larmoyante *hope of* Santa Maria Della Salute *and the desperate dignity of* Nevermore, *repeating them alternately. But in these hundred-odd verses there are also Pound, Mann, Selimović, Murano glass, labyrinths made of mirrors, Byron, Dürer, Titian, canals and gondolas, pigeons and seagulls, Shylock, the ambiguous Bridge of Sighs, and Nostradamus, or that prophecy of his in which as proof of the power of the new Attila (in which people* post festum *recognized Hitler), he says that he would even rule* over Venice.

The book begins of course with that memorable prologue:

By the sharp white edge of a pier
Floats the vague silhouette of a ship
Dusky bluish light of pain
Like the celebrated lighthouse of Rhodes

Like the sounds of Pyotr's B minor
Endless sentiment—gendered feeling
Passion is not a matter of gender but of pain
Brodsky wrote the truth.

It was as if my friend foretold Brodsky's passion for Venice and quoted, in the context of Venice, his verse written before Brodsky had even seen Venice. I will reveal a secret to you—in the year of the publication of his last collection my friend was godfather to my first granddaughter and he named her Venisa. In this book for the first time he writes prose poems like the one titled "Pain" where he says:

The question of gender is one of those famous grammatical conundrums. The concepts masculinum, femininum *(and sometimes* neutrum *too) are unavoidable parts of every language textbook. An old professor of French said that all bad things are of the feminine gender. But in our language pain is a noun that can be both masculine and feminine. But even pain is defeated by this city that in our language can be feminine (Venecija), masculine (Venedik),*[14] *and plural (Mleci).*[15]

And Muhamed's only somewhat political poem, the controversial "Marshal," is also written in prose:

Even in the time of McLuhan's global village *our own language and immediate surroundings are our primary determinants. Because Mr. McLuhan is not the first person I think of when the word Marshal is mentioned.*

You know that today some people call this poem "Ode to a Dictator," and those same people used—while Muhamed was on his deathbed—to call it *shameful irony.* My friend—as you know—died in 1982 in Venedik.

Well—perhaps you are wondering—why I am writing all of this to you? Why am I—like the friend whom I have never stopped mourning—*jumping up and down* saying I will not write about personal, deeply intimate things, and yet still writing a letter like this to an unknown man? Do you remember what I said at the beginning? I am writing to you because there was no *proverbial conflict between life and work* in my friend's case. My friend lived the way he wrote, but—consciously or unconsciously—he built his *image* differently. Why? For years I myself have wondered that and I believe I have found the reason. Were I a religious man I would say that God wanted to make him resemble our vision of the archetypical poet. But, given that, in the narrow religious sense, like my friend (who once wrote

I do not kneel to you, God
Nor do I kiss your robe
Because for me you are an essence
An essence that is loosing its attributes)

I am not a believer, I cannot say that. Still, Muhamed's ancestors were believers—great believers—God-seekers, and some of that must have remained in him. (At the end of life he liked to quote Wallace Stevens: *After we disavowed belief in God, poetry became the essence that replaced it as life's salvation.*) He is in fact a grotesque continuation of the dervishes and sufias,[16] the last seeker of the absolute. And are we not all in our own way exactly that? I think here about my own political adventure and about that passion of yours to interpret and explain everything. But still you ask: even if Muhamed seeks the absolute, why did this have to be absent from his public image, the *image* seen and remembered by the majority? That I do not know. Perhaps he was simply a shy man, perhaps strange in some way, and perhaps his unconscious (which is a new name for what used to be called the mystical influence) did not want to betray the canon law of his ancestors. I do not know—as I said—but I do know that I am getting older and that I won't do so much longer, and I know that more and more frequently I imagine that the large neon advertising sign under my window—an oval mosaic of small round lights that looks like a plastic model of molecular DNA—is actually Ramadan lights and more and more often I think that the gun whose shot marks noon is in fact the announcement of iftar.[17]

Translated from the Bosnian by Oleg Andrić and Andrew Wachtel

■ □ ■ □ ■

THE HOT SUN'S GOLDEN CIRCLE

IN THE DAYS OF THE GLORIOUS AND WELL-KNOWN EIGHTEENTH dynasty, the dynasty that turned Egypt into a world empire, fourteen centuries before Christ, a young pharaoh ascended the Egyptian throne in Thebes, a young pharaoh who was at first named Amenhotep, like his father, Amenhotep IV. During the celebrated reigns of his ancestors, wide spaces of Nubia to the south and Palestine, Syria, and a part of Mesopotamia to the north had been annexed to the Egyptian empire. The young Amenhotep IV preserved the great legacy of four Tutmoses, his three namesakes, as well as Queen Hatshepsut. An immense land stretching from Kush and the Sudan to the Euphrates and beyond the Euphrates was under his scepter. In Luxor near Thebes his divine father, Amenhotep III, had raised a magnificent temple dedicated to the ithyphallic Amon-Ra, a temple whose richly carved columns, even today, make shadows under the sun on the red-hot desert sand, a temple connected to the Great Temple in Karnak by an alley of sphinxes. Next to them on the western bank of the Nile, chiseled into the rock, were the royal burial temples, or pharaohs' graves. Dead pharaohs were often deified and their graves were given the markings of temples. In addition to pharaohs, some viziers, like the great Imhotep, were declared gods. Thus Amenhotep son of Hapu, vizier at the court of Amenhotep III, a warrior, builder, adviser, and learned man who *edited all holy books and saw Thoth's outline,* was declared a god upon his death, and Amenhotep III dedicated a sculpture to him in Karnak. Various divine creations were worshipped all over the Egyptian empire, fertility, birth and death, and holy animals: many holy bulls, rams, crocodiles, and holy birds, and then the cat, the rabbit, the dog, the jackal, and the scarab. But still among all of these countless divine creatures there had to exist a kind of hierarchy, some kind of division of power among the various divine creatures with one supreme god and the many gods under him, with a narrow top and a wide bottom like a pyramid. At that time the supreme god was Amon-Ra, a god created through the amalgamation of the great god of the city of Thebes, Amon, and the ancient deity Ra. Amon-Ra was embodied as a goose, a ram, a man with blue-black skin, and it was said that he could take on any possible shape. In paintings and statues Amon-Ra was often depicted with the facial features of one of the pharaohs. In many statues, for example, Amon-Ra has the face of Amenhotep III, the father of the young pharaoh Amenhotep IV.

Amenhotep IV was a tall and skinny man with a long neck, large ears and nose, and black somewhat curly hair. His skin was decidedly pale. He was not, like most of his ancestors, inclined to be a warrior or a hunter, nor did he have a strong predilection for pharaonic luxury. His royal nature was reflected more in a purely intellectual and spiritual interest in the greatness of the Egyptian empire and in the varied characteristics of its subjects. Perhaps one of the reasons for this was the fact that his beloved wife Nefertiti was a Syrian princess, and Amenhotep's enchantment with her Asian beauty led to an interest in her homeland as well as in other regions of earth unknown to him but with populations subservient to him, the pharaoh. Because now the whole world known to Egyptians was under the pharaoh's rule, and Thebes, the city of Amon and the seat of the pharaoh's throne, was the center of the world. The primarily spiritual interests of Amenhotep IV were reflected in his interest in religious questions as well. He had had frequent talks with many of Amon-Ra's priests at the pharaoh's court even in the period when his father was on the throne and he was still a boy. At that time he had talked gladly with Amenhotep son of Hapu, vizier at his father's court. Vizier Amenhotep, as a learned and literary man, was particularly inclined toward Thoth, the scribe of the gods, the discoverer of speech, a deity embodied as an ibis-headed man wearing a half-moon and ring, or as a dog-headed baboon. With his praises of Thoth, praises he heard from the vizier Amenhotep, the boy Amenhotep IV would often anger Amon-Ra's priests, just as he would anger his namesake the vizier by mentioning Amon-Ra's magnificence and sacredness. A child's mind always looks for clear answers and clear coordinates. Amenhotep was confused by the different incarnations and different representations of the gods. Amon-Ra could be a goose, a ram, or a blue-black man, but also anything else, and, what is more, some priests considered him the god of water, others the god of fertility, and some others the god who made decisions about time and the seasons, while the priests of his Great Temple in Karnak considered him the god of the wind. It was similar with Thoth and with the other gods. Thoth was a dog-headed baboon, an ibis-headed man, the Lord of Magic, a lotus flower, and the seeker for truth in the large dispute between Horus and Seth. Horus and Seth had, of course, many personifications and characteristics of their own as well as many relationships with other gods who also had no shortage of characteristics and incarnations and relationships with new divine creatures. Even the boy's frequent interlocutor, Amenhotep son of Hapu, became a god upon his death and entered into complicated relationships with Thoth and Osiris. So the mystic pyramid of Egyptian theology was still growing although the large stone pyramids in Giza, the tombs of the ancient pharaohs, had been raised and completed a long time before.

After marrying Nefertiti, Amenhotep IV often entered into peculiar theological discussions with her. His marriage was a rare fusion of love with state as well as family interest, a fusion so rare that it *belongs among those things, like colossal sea snakes, that we are not sure whether they exist only in fables or somewhere in reality.* Nefertiti's stories about the Syrian gods of her childhood brought additional turmoil and confusion into the already complex private and intimate cosmogony of the young pharaoh. And turmoil and confusion regularly lead to doubt. Amenhotep IV began to doubt. And doubt is a thankless thing, something that almost never stops halfway, and knows neither pause nor mercy.

Like a spoiled child Amenhotep IV began to test the power and vengefulness of certain gods. Since he despised war, he decided to despise Mentu, the pharaohs' warrior god usually depicted in the shape of a bull-headed man with a bow and arrows, and mace and knife, or in the shape of a man with a falcon's feather. He ordered the dissolution of Mentu's cult, explaining it by the need to confirm peace in the Egyptian empire through the disappearance of the warrior god. This pharaoh's whim, though considered very strange, did not cause strong reactions. Every pharaoh is capricious and they are all given to somewhat bizarre moves, proving by them, perhaps, their own regal divine nature. When by accident a ruler's whims coincide with the people's interest, then that ruler is declared generous and a benefactor. For the military victories of Tutmose III, which had broadened the borders of the empire, and the many building works of Amenhotep III, which cheered the Egyptians, were in their essence just pharaohs' whims as well. And every man is inclined to have varied whims but only a pharaoh has the power to realize his whims and turn them into fact. *Chaque fou a sa marotte.* This caprice of Amenhotep IV could, at its core, seem pretty reasonable for a pharaoh, because pharaohs often, while still alive, considered themselves already gods, *the creators of all things.* On one papyrus it says that the difference between gods and pharaohs is smaller than the difference between a pharaoh and his subjects. After dissolving Mentu's cult, Amenhotep IV impatiently and almost longingly waited for negative consequences and punishment. But nothing happened.

Encouraged by the easy victory, the pharaoh continued. Like a sparrow hawk who steals a chicken and then proudly circles above a herd of sheep prepared to steal a lamb, Amenhotep IV targeted a new and bigger prize, not a lamb but a true ram, the holy divine ram from Mendes depicted with horizontal and wavy horns sitting on a throne, a judge intermediary in the dispute between Horus and Seth. He dissolved the cult of Mendes' ram. Although the people of Mendes considered this blasphemy, in Thebes and other cities this act seemed pretty innocuous, but even then some of the priests there already started asking whether the pharaoh intended to stop. And the pharaoh waited for bad news from Mendes. There was no bad news.

Numerous practical and experiential confirmations of a feeling demand a theoretical intellectual explanation. The fulfillment of a foreboding seeks an elucidation. Experiences are just the building blocks of the metaphysical house of one's own worldview. Something that without a vision is just an irresponsible game becomes a revolutionary program when it acquires a vision. So, the momentary cessation of the pharaoh's dissolution whims, which some saw as the result of oversaturation and fulfillment, was in fact just a pause during which doubt solidified, taking its seat again—a seat that had temporarily been occupied by immature nihilistic trances. It was a period of composure and thinking, a period during which the pharaoh observed his own acts through the optics of his own feeling of the world, a feeling that was slowly being distilled from a murky liquid of dreams, fears, inclinations, and hopes, a period similar to the development of a photograph in a dark room when the photograph, which had to be made in the light, gets contours for which darkness is necessary, a period similar to the sorting of childhood memories by an adult man when a man, from seemingly random experiences, chooses characteristic moments and acts as an itinerary on a road of the creation of his own adult character. Simply speaking, it was a calm before the storm.

Amenhotep IV began searching through ancient papyruses looking for the root of modern superstitions (because every false belief is a superstition) in the ancient legends and faraway misty spaces of ancient times. He slowly began to realize that the kinships and similarities of different gods had their roots, in fact, in the separation of an ancient single god (like when a worm is cut in the middle and the two identical halves each go to their own side), just as the seemingly incoherent characteristics and competences of one god had their roots, in fact, in the amalgamation of two originally completely different gods (like when the fairground magicians show a calf with a sheep's head)—Amon-Ra represented an example of such an amalgamation. With such a discovery before the young pharaoh's eyes, the whole complex structure of beliefs and convictions that had arched over him since childhood, that had also arched over every citizen of Egypt, his every subject and the whole Egyptian empire, began to crumble. If there is no Mentu, who, then, brought martial luck to his ancestors? If Mendes' ram does not exist, who was the judge intermediary in the dispute between Horus and Seth? There was no dispute. There is no Horus or Seth. If there is no Horus and Seth, who else does not exist? Or, rather, who does?

For some time the young pharaoh behaved like the members of Pythagoras's school, who, when they discovered irrational numbers or when they realized that the square root of two cannot be represented as a ratio of two numbers, or rather, cannot be written as a fraction, hid that as the worst possible secret. Because for the Pythagoreans this represented something that completely changed their view of the world, something that subjected their axiomatic view of numeric relationships as the foundation of the universe to radical criticism. Analogously, for the Egyptians the gods represented the creative and moving power of the universe. How would it be possible to tell them that there are no gods? To take away one or two gods meant to take away two small stones from the foundation of the great pyramid—something almost unnoticeable, but if one kept taking small stones away in the end the pyramid would tumble. Not long after one disloyal Pythagorean spread the fatal fact about the square root of two, that traitor drowned in the sea. Pythagoreans considered this the gods' punishment. Amenhotep IV was in an even more thankless situation. He was alone with his dark discovery. He was the only possible traitor. And even if something were to happen to him after a possible treason, to whom could he assign the blame?

But Amenhotep IV could not be completely confident in this whole newly created confusion that devastated his mind and heart. He had gotten into a crisis of meaning, but he could not see how to get out of it. But if he did not have signposts and lighthouses in books that would ease his fight through his present darkness and desert with carved signs and ancient lanterns, he did have something else: a smart woman who loved him. In the darkness of the royal bed, the pharaoh confided to his wife. He spoke for a long time: at first slowly, with restraint and seeming calm as if talking about something that did not touch him personally, but then quickly and disconnectedly with many gesticulations, with uncontrolled raising and lowering of his voice in a soliloquy in which enthusiasm and pain were fused in the same way that in the form of goddess Mertseger a woman and a cobra were fused. Nefertiti was silent, listening to him carefully without sighs and interjections. Just when the pharaoh finally fell silent, his wife recalled a memory from her early youth in her homeland. A long-haired young man came from an unknown region to the court of her father and announced that the cohort of gods whom Syria worshipped was in fact just a heap of shaped clay. Asked what gods he relied on, the young man answered that he believed in only one, his own god. *Then let that god help you now*—the court hangmen said before they executed him. *There is one god, there is one god, but which one?*—the lost young pharaoh repeated while dawn broke in Thebes and while the first rays of sun caressed his face and tickled his eyes.

When a man confirms that a premise he considered sure is in fact wrong and that with elimination of that mistake everything fits perfectly, that is how the pharaoh must have felt. Surrounded by a legion of gods since childhood, the only alternative to him seemed a strong and radical *either/or* differentiation: either a plurality of gods or no gods—an irresolvable conflict of his ancestors' dogma and his own realizations, which could only end miraculously. In the seventeenth century one Jesuit astronomer published a book that tried to refute Copernicus's teachings, teachings that he thought highly of, by the way, because they overlapped with his own observations. But the Bible is insistent: *The earth is made in such a way that it cannot revolve.* Respecting the Holy Testament, he claimed that the earth is the unmovable center of the universe, around which the moon, the sun, Jupiter, and Saturn revolve, but the three remaining planets, Mercury, Venus, and Mars, do not revolve around the earth, but around the sun. The strange mélange of the teachings of Charles Darwin and the Lord, an unusual combination of *The Origin of Species* and the Bible, which claims that fossils of evolutionary shapes are not a result of complex geological processes but a result of direct divine creation, is yet another related example of such a danger, a danger that Amenhotep IV avoided with the help of his wife. But to know what is being looked for still does not mean that it has been found. Amenhotep IV was still looking, he still did not see his god.

But how to recognize a god other than by his attributes? Amenhotep IV knew only one attribute of his god: oneness. How can oneness be applied to those natural forces deified by Egyptians when all of the natural forces are unique? But, in addition to oneness, it is possible to assign majesty to every god, and thus, to Amenhotep IV's god as well. What is one and majestic? The sun. The Pharaoh had to know that Egypt did not lack sun gods, but there could not be only one sun and a plurality of sun gods. In ancient papyruses the pharaoh found an almost-forgotten symbol, the symbol of an almost-forgotten god, a symbol of the sun at its zenith, clear and hot in a shape of a red circle whose rays reach the earth. That was a picture of his god. It was Aton. Aton was the young pharaoh's god, the only and true god.

Soon the pharaoh gathered all of the courtiers, all of the highly ranked officials, and all of the priests from all the temples of Egypt at his court. All of them must have known something was happening. The pharaoh ordered all present to gather in front of the court at dawn. When the large bloody sphere started rising over Thebes, pouring in shiny jets its benevolent light on the Nile and the sand, the pharaoh stepped in front of his subjects and spoke to them as follows.

Egyptian people, there is no god but Aton, Aton is the only god. There is but one sun that rises every morning to illuminate one Egyptian state, one Nile and one desert. There is but one pharaoh. There is one life, one death, and one wife given to all of us, and one god. And that god is Aton. Do not lie to yourselves, people, and do not rave because this imaginary bestiary purportedly deserving of respect has no purpose, it is a bestiary imposed on you, a bestiary imposed on you by you yourself. Nun, Ra, Kherpi, Shu, Tefnut, Anhur, Geb, Nut, Osiris, Isis, Seth, Nephthys, Horus, Har, Horus Behedti, Harakhte, Harmakhis, Harseisis, Hathor, Anubis, Upuant, Thoth, Seshat, Nekhbet, Buto, Harsafes, Mentu, Sebek, Amon, Khons, Mut, Bastet, Neith, Ptah, Sekhmet, Nefertem, Khnum, Heket, Satis, Anuket, Hapi, Min, Bes, Tawaret, Meskhet, Renenet, Shai, Hathor, Seker, Serket, Hu, Sia, Sakhmet, and Heh and all the other purported gods, all the dead pharaohs, all the purported holy animals, it is all a huge lie, a huge pile of lies. And I am a king who lives in truth. And thus I tell you: Aton is the only god. And his picture is this sun that rises, the sun that gives us life and life's joy. Do not fool yourselves, people, and do not place your hopes in rams and cows, in snakes and crocodiles, in herons and hawks, in cats and dogs, in the dead known and unknown, in invented visions of your fears, in that freakish gallery of randomly and monstrously assembled heads, trunks, legs, arms, and wings: in hermaphrodite frogs, in snake-headed men, in men with frogs' heads, in bearded men with ostrich feathers on their heads, in Typhoeus animals, in women with lions' heads, in horned young men, in anthropomorphic gods with the heads of lizards and falcons, in golden hawks with herons' heads, in goddesses in the shape of cows, in black pigs, in monkeys with dogs' heads, in crocodiles with horns, in mummified hawks, in freakish dwarfs, in gravid hippopotamuses that have a lion's legs and a crocodile's tail, do not rely on these hybrids, these miscarried babies, these fruits of dread and insecurity that can be met only in dreams, do not wail over graves, do not kneel in front of colors, stones, and clay, do not pray to jackals and scarabs.

The pharaoh stopped for a moment. The masses observed him silently, shocked and thunderstruck. The sun shone goldenly and squandered its rays generously, as if in confirmation of the pharaoh's words. Everything must have looked truly unreal. The mass of Amon-Ra's priests glanced at each other in disbelief. As if hearing their unspoken arguments, the pharaoh continued speaking.

But lies have permeated us and it will be difficult to defeat them. Lies are in our blood, in our eyes, in our ears, lies are in our hearts, in our cemeteries, in our books, lies are in our pictures, our sculptures, in our houses, lies are in our beds, at our tables, in our temples, and finally—this is the worst—lies are in our language, in our poems, and our names. Nonexistent Amon grins viciously even from my name, but no longer. Henceforth I kneel to the only god with my name too, to Aton, and from today I use a name that describes my essence, no longer a name that has been a nonexistent shadow of something that does not exist, from today I am the one who serves Aton, from today I am Akhenaton. Today I am ordering the closing of all temples devoted to nonexistent gods, I am ordering the deletion of all the names of nonexistent gods from all stele and walls, I am ordering the deletion of all names of the dead pharaohs, my ancestors, if they contain in themselves the name of a nonexistent god, the same way my previous name contained it, I am ordering the cessation of every practice of adoration of shameful fabrications until today considered gods. I am ordering sun and truth. I am ordering this in the name of Aton. Oh, you, the only god, next to whom no other exists. Oh, living Aton, glory be to you!

The pharaoh's determination was not exhausted in shiny rhetoric. Everything he announced he began to carry out without delay. But the reception given to this revolution by his subjects was far from delighted. The new religion got sincere believers only among the pharaoh's closest retinue, among his most loyal courtiers. The people of Thebes, prodded by the oppressed priests of the abolished cult of Amon-Ra, continued mostly with their old superstitions and idolatry. Because it was difficult to shed the invisible web of the imaginary polytheistic museum, which, in fact, had played more of a ritual, traditional, and nostalgic role than a metaphysical one in people's lives. It was difficult to accept the cruel singularity of a new religion that deprives a person of the possibility, if he errs toward one god or is scorned for no reason by some other god, to find solace in the embrace of some other god. It was difficult to understand the radical iconoclasm of the new religion toward any painting or plastic representation of Aton. Every visual representation of Aton, other than the symbolic representation of the sun's disk, was banned. Akhenaton said that god does not have a shape. And finally, it was difficult to resign oneself to the negation of the kingdom of the dead and otherworldly existence. Akhenaton said that it was a lie to say that death is not the end. And although the names of the abolished cohort of idols no longer surfaced on the temples and the walls, they continued to live in the houses of Thebes. Thebes did not worship Aton.

Akhenaton's disinclination toward any use of military force was proportional to his awareness of the fact that—among everything else—the loyalty of the people of Thebes to Amon-Ra was a consequence of his local mythological foundation. Because the first member of this duo, this amalgamated supreme divinity, Amon, was in fact an ancient city god of Thebes, and the people of Thebes believed that it was due to him that they became the center of the empire. As a result, the pharaoh had to know that without employing means he did not want to use, Thebes, at least during the lives of this generation, meaning during his life too, would not belong to Aton. But he who declared himself *a king who lives in truth* perhaps did not want to spend his life in a city of lies. Akhenaton perhaps thought about moving the court to some other city, but all the Egyptian cities had their own city gods and their own local mythology. What could he do other than found a new city?

On the Nile, downstream from Thebes, Akhenaton, applying the poetics of that Egyptian religion that he despised, anticipatorily unifying in himself Romulus and Mohammed, making a mélange of beginnings of time of future calendars and achieving a unification of *hijra*[1] and *ab urbe condita,* taking his beliefs, his family, retinue, and courtiers to the city he himself founded, to Akhetaton, the city of Aton's horizon. Under the fertile sun, the city grew quickly, the city that worshipped Aton. It was a city without temples dedicated to false gods, a city without a circus on its frescos and without an imaginary bestiary of sculptures. When he finally completed the last tasks there, Akhenaton devoted himself almost completely to his family: to his wife and daughters (he would have a total of six, and no sons). He wrote poems and hymns to Aton.

Oh, living Aton, the beginning of life
Creator of a germ in a woman
And a seed in a man
You who give the breath of life
To all that you created

How many are your deeds
And they are hidden from us
Oh only god whose power
No one else has

To all in the heights
That fly with their wings
You give all that is needed

How beautiful your symbols are
Oh the lord of eternity
In the heaven there is a Nile for strangers
And a treasure for all countries

You dawn you glow you go far away
And you return
Dissolved in infinite number of shapes
But you remain one always

You created strange countries
As well as the Egyptian land
You placed every man
In his own place
People speak many languages

In bodies and complexion
They are different
In order to differentiate people
From people

No one knows you
But your son Akhenaton
To whom you gave wisdom
In your thoughts and your power

Akhenaton was still the pharaoh under whose scepter was the whole empire of Egypt. But the tall tower of peace, whose foundations had been dug by his ancestors through wars, began to crumble. Warlike tribes from the edge of the world endangered the border regions of the empire. Those areas were almost unpopulated, but while they were in Egyptian hands, they secured the inner parts of empire. The people of Thebes, like evil-omened birds, quietly croaked that Mentu was taking revenge on the unfaithful pharaoh. The generals were waiting for that moment when they would, under the pharaoh's command, march toward the borders to confirm Egyptian dominance, but that moment did not come. Akhenaton consciously accepted the crumbling of the empire in the name of peace. This was not just about the pharaoh's personal indisposition toward war, because had it been, the war could have been led by his command but without the need for his active participation. But to Akhenaton war was a double evil since the deaths in his army as well as in the enemy's were equally odious. All people are the children of Aton.

Akhetaton, the city of Aton's horizon, even if it was not built from ivory in a metaphorical sense, represented a grandiose ivory tower. Because Akhenaton's move did not lessen Theban intolerance toward the pharaoh and new religion, but it in fact increased it. The high officials of Thebes plotted whispered conspiracies, aware they would not carry them out, but just to give vent to their hatred. But the majority of the people of Akhetaton were formerly Thebans, and the people of Thebes knew that they had followed the pharaoh out of greed, and that their loyalty to both Aton and Akhenaton was dishonest and hypocritical. On top of all, the latest news from the borders created a stir even in the army, which traditionally was loyal to the rulers, so that the citizens of Thebes, and especially Amon-Ra's priests, rubbed their hands with satisfaction while spitefully enquiring about Akhenaton's health.

Seventeen years after ascending the throne, the pharaoh Akhenaton died. Perhaps in the moment of death he was able to look at Aton's face without squinting. He was succeeded by his son-in-law Tutankhaton, better known as Tutankhamen, because he returned the capital to Thebes and replaced Aton's name in his own name with Amon's. Amon-Ra's cult ruled again, the old polytheistic bestiary returned to the temples. Aton's and Akhenaton's names were erased from all memorials, and Akhetaton, the city of Aton's horizon, was destroyed, burned, and robbed. The ruins of Akhenaton's capital are called Tel el Amarna today. In Tel el Amarna an empty tomb of Akhenaton was found. No one knows what happened to the mummy, but perhaps it is a better posthumous destiny to have a cenotaph than a mummy, that eternally deceiving pawn of eternity or posthumous remains, a pinch of ashes, a pile of long bones and a Hamletian skull. Also, no one knows what happened to Aton's religion. Perhaps it was buried forever in the empty pharaoh's grave, or perhaps some loyal subject of Akhenaton named Ramses or Tutmose deleted the name of the nonexistent god Ra or Thoth from his own name and thus, becoming Moses or Mosis, found new believers whom he then led from Egypt. Aton's acts are unpredictable. *Oh, living Aton, glory be to you!*

Translated from the Bosnian by Oleg Andrić and Andrew Wachtel

■ □ ■ □ ■

A TWILIGHT ENCOUNTER

The Ambiguity of Boring History

Rousseau's sentence *Fortunate are a people whose history is boring to read* is usually interpreted as a desire for an absence of wars, unrest, floods. However, it is also possible that boredom might be a manifestation of a persistent and monotonous repetition of similar events even though those events are not boring as such. What I want to say is that the monotony of the endless repetition of unpleasant events does not have that same lightness as the boredom that led to the exodus from Eden, and that is, together with leisure, a faithful companion of happiness. But since man calls destiny only what pounds him, even though fortuitous circumstances are fruits of destiny, too, boredom is generally perceived only as the monotony of pleasant events. People like to invoke Tolstoy's words that only misfortunes are unique while all happiness is identical, that unhappy families and countries are each unhappy in their own way. Heine would not have agreed with Tolstoy. According to him, every tragedy is *familiengluck.* The Bosnian tragedy is a tragedy of being stretched: on the east it is a wild frontier and rebellious bulwark, on the west a devil's island and the dark side of the moon.

The Weight of Smoke

However, the ambiguity of boredom is not the only historical ambiguity. All of history is an ambiguity of a sort. Each nation has its own history. The realization of Russell's *Let the people think* is as unattainable as is his old countryman's state whose unreachable nature is hidden within its very name: Utopia. A hero is always a perpetrator too. An English nobleman and a famous navigator is a pirate and a thief to the Spaniards. It is only certain that he brought tobacco to Europe and that he managed to measure the weight of smoke, first by weighing a cigarette and then subtracting the weight of the butt along with the weight of the ashes once he had finished the cigarette. Tobacco was brought to Bosnia as an agricultural commodity by Ali-Pasha Rizvanbegović, a Herzegovinian Sultan and a Montenegrin butcher, the sworn enemy of Prince-bishop Petar Petrović Njegoš II, the Montenegrin Solomon and a poet of slaughter.

Wilkinson

Belted, and carrying a sword, according to an honorable family tradition (whose ironic counterpoint as well as whose seamy side is evident from the razor industry logo), Gardner Wilkinson, while traveling through Herzegovina and Montenegro, took upon himself the noble task of mediating between Ali-Pasha and Njegoš, hoping to abolish that ugly and primitive custom of decapitation wherein heads later serve as trophies. Wilkinson describes the origins of his commendable urge in the following words: *I admit that after I came to Cetinje, and after I saw twenty Turkish heads, a very sincere desire to abolish decapitation overwhelmed me. That feeling remained strong after I saw the same cruel trophies in Mostar.* After a conversation he had with Ali-Pasha, Wilkinson wrote to Njegoš, *I also explained to him that customs like this one make a war even more desperate—giving it a quality that our wars do not have.* But both Njegoš and Ali-Pasha remained deaf when it came to Wilkinson's cries as if the possibility of losing their own heads in an equally concrete and metaphoric register provided them with a kind of much-needed cold dispassionateness—almost pleasure.

They say that Njegoš, while looking at his reflection in a baroque Venetian mirror, recited the appropriate verses under his breath:

Black moustache where will you suffer
In Mostar or in Travnik?

(It is quite another thing that, according to Wilkinson, decapitation was something utterly alien to Western European civilization, but that only few decades separated him from the revolutionary havoc in the streets of Paris, the guillotines, and the barbarism of crowds tossing severed heads around.)

A Historical Note

Whose were those twenty heads Wilkinson talks about? Whose heads were on display in that unique Cetinje exhibit? Perhaps the heads belonged to Ali-Pasha's emissaries who had been sent to negotiate with Njegoš and were later decapitated by the prince-bishop's men who ambushed, tricked, and killed the victims in a place called Bašina Voda? They murdered all the beys except for one, taking their heads as trophies. But their leader, Bey Resulbegović, was not among them. He had stayed behind in Nikšić feigning illness, just like a high school student would do, and saved his head. According to tradition, Resulbegović's salvation should be ascribed to something else. It is ascribed to a conversation at twilight.

Riders and a Prophet

A line of highborn horsemen moved slowly through the cruel landscape of Herzegovinian rocks. They had already been traveling for a few days and still had a few days to go before they arrived. One could sense the sun at its zenith, hellish heat, crickets buzzing (like the winding of millions of wristwatches, as the poet with a prophetic name put it), the remote murmur of a river, stale air, tired horses, sweat on turban-swathed foreheads, half-closed eyes, dry lips, the rhythmic stamping of hoofs, moist hands holding the reins, the outlines of the mountains, a delicate foretaste of twilight. Parallel with the sunset in the west, the strange silhouette of a tall, slender man who walked leaning on a long cane made of yew appeared against the eastern horizon. As he approached, his face became more and more visible, revealing its characteristic features, blue sleepy eyes, a large long forehead, a yellowish untrimmed beard, a long thin mustache, pale rolled-back lips. He was about sixty. He walked around in ragged clothes, like a beggar. He was barefoot. By now everybody should have recognized him. His name was Mate Glušac; legends about him are still alive all across Herzegovina. It is said that he was born in the village of Korita in 1774. He lived alone helping the baptized and the unbaptized, he practiced magic, cured, and told fortunes. According to folk legends, he never owned a house, never got married, always fasted and read prayers. There was about him something of an Old Testament Hebrew prophet's passion, he was esoteric like Celtic druids, his mysticism resembled that of the sorcerers in *The Arabian Nights,* he was as picturesque as John the Baptist, ascetic as a monk, magical as a shaman, immersed in faith like a dervish, charismatic as a rock-and-roll idol, poor as the ancient Franciscans, powerful as a tribal medicine man, he had the dignity of a priest, the shameful respect of a lunatic, and the tranquility of a wise old man from Chinese fairy tales.

A Dramatic Omen

Bey Resulbegović greeted his old acquaintance with a smile. *It's great to see you in good health, Mate.*

Mate returned his greeting with the simplicity and spontaneity of a feebleminded man. *Where are you headed, Bey?*

To see Prince-bishop Njegoš in Montenegro, Ali-Pasha sends us—the bey replied in a slightly lowered voice, imitating anger as if he were speaking to a child.

Mate's eyes widened; he looked off somewhere in the distance, behind the bey, and began speaking quickly as if reciting a previously memorized text. *Listen to me, Bey, you will not see the prince-bishop nor will you talk to him, and all but one person will see him from two places. From the first place they will talk and look at each other for an hour or two. From the second place they will look at each other for exactly two months until their eyes fall out of their sockets.*

Now both the bey and Mate Glušac were silent. After some time, the bey asked Mate as if he were in a trance, *What did you just say, Mate?*

Mate's face relaxed, his gaze became crystal clear. *Nothing, my bey, and if I said something, I don't remember it anymore.*

Mate then continued on his way without looking back like some desired but unreachable and undoubting Orpheus, while the bey, on horseback, stared after him for a long time looking like a sculpture made of salt or Eurydice on Pegasus.

The Phenomenology of Twilight

Twilight suddenly trampled the field. Darkness lengthens shadows and contributes powerfully to the grayness. Night gives a certain dimension to words and things that they do not have during daylight.

Yin replaces Yang—the Chinese would say.

The heartbeat slows, the blood pressure drops, it is the time of parasimpaticus—doctors would say.

Infantile fears awake along with the instincts inherited from our ancestors—claim psychoanalysts.

The Twilight Zone—announces the television.

Morning is wiser than evening—repeat the village wise men.

There is no sorrow like evening sorrow—wails an oriental love song.

A poet reveals: *Darkness is the blood of wounded things.*

Another poet adds: *Girls sing at dusk.*

The Salvational Effect of Superstition

It would be as unrewarding to guess the bey's thoughts as it would be to evaluate the effect the prophecy had on his decision to remain in Nikšić. The fact is that he stayed in Nikšić while the other beys continued their journey with its well-known ending in Bašina Voda where they talked to the prince-bishop for *an hour or two.* The heads of all the beys except for one (who was most probably spared to play the role of ill-fated Philippides) were taken to Cetinje and there they were able to look at Njegoš for *exactly two months* until their eyes fell out of their sockets. Two months may be the exact time period needed for eyes to fall out of severed heads. Perhaps it would be interesting to imagine what would have happened had Bey Resulbegović not taken the warning into account and not remained in Nikšić. Would he have been saved anyway? It is hard to imagine that the Philipedean role would have fallen to him just because he was the highest-ranked nobleman among the emissaries. But calling Mate's prophecy a warning seems equally wrong. This is not the case of Caesar and the Ides of March. Mate did not advise Bey Rasulbegović to be careful; he simply read his future as if it had been written on his palm. In the end, this legend resembles the English tale according to which the clairvoyant peasant Robert

Nixon foretold Henry IV's victory over Richard II. That prophecy took place during their crucial battle, but it was uttered hundreds of kilometers away from the battlefield, in a remote village where no one even knew about the battle. (In his book *Prediction and Prophecy* Keith Alis mentions this story.) Still, the encounter between Mate Glušac and Bey Resulbegović differs from that English story because Robert Nixon's role is that of a spectator who does not interact with the protagonists. It is also different than the Ides of March because it does not offer a choice. Mate Glušac is as merciless as destiny. But the question arises: would something else have stopped the bey had it not been for Mate? Would what was predicted have had to happen regardless of the manner in which events unfolded, or did the implicit warning in the prophecy ensure its own realization? Did Mate address the bey because he was grateful for his kindness and thus save him? Was the prediction just a reading of something previously written or was it a correction that led to salvation? Whatever it was, because he remained in Nikšić, the bey remained alive. *And this is the benefit of superstition and that benefit should not be belittled.*

A Final Note

Mate Glušac was ninety-six when he died. It is said that he foretold his own death as well. He is buried near the Church of Saint Tekla in Danilovgrad. There is no marker on his grave. Instead, an enormous tree grows there, more than three feet in diameter. Prince-bishop Petar II Petrović Njegoš and Ali-Pasha Rizvanbegović both died in 1851. From a historical point of view they died at the same moment; like enemies exhausted from fighting or pairs of mythical unhappy lovers. The encyclopedias available to me at the moment mention neither Resulbegović nor Wilkinson. However, the genius who wrote *Die Welt Als Wille und Vorstellung* in the *Second Volume* points out the inadequacy of those encyclopedias by mentioning the very same Mister Wilkinson in a footnote. In so doing, Arthur Schopenhauer granted me a rare compliment. Because in the same footnote he quoted the *London Times,* and he pointed out even more clearly, more subtly, and in more detail the *strange and mysterious solace* mentioning, along with everything else, the contours of *feu follet, which summon vain and lonely sensibilities in moments of illumination.*

Postscriptum

After this story was published for the first time, I read a book that mentions, among others, Bey Resulbegović, whom I had come to think of as a mythological character as I could not find his name anywhere. The book is titled *Crystal Bars,* written by the man to whom *The Knife with the Rosewood Handle* is dedicated.

Translated from the Bosnian by Nikola Petković and Andrew Wachtel

■ □ ■ □ ■

THE STORY OF TWO BROTHERS

Abel was a keeper of sheep but Cain was a tiller of the Ground. . . . And Cain talked with his brother: but it came to pass when they were in the field that Cain rose up against his brother, and slew him. And the Lord said unto Cain, Where is Abel thy brother? And he said: I know not: Am I my brother's keeper? And He said: What hast thou done? The voice of thy brother's blood crieth unto me from the ground. . . . And Cain went out from the presence of the Lord, and dwelt in the Land of Nod, on the East of Eden.

The Book of Genesis

This is the age-old tale of two brothers in a new and solemn form. Ever since the world began there have been two rival brothers, constantly born anew. One is older, wiser, stronger, closer to the world, to real life and everything that links and motivates the majority of people, a man who succeeds in everything, who always knows what should and what should not be done, what can be asked both of others and of himself. The second is his exact opposite. A man of brief span, ill fortune, and a misguided first step, a man whose ambitions constantly bypass what is needed and surpass what is possible. In his conflict with his elder brother—and conflict is inevitable—he has lost the battle before it begins.

Ivo Andrić, *The Damned Yard*

AN EMPHATIC PROPHECY OF SCHILLER, EMBRACED BY BOTH BEETHOVEN and the European Union, proclaims: *Alle menschen werden bruden.* This festive fraternization will occur *under the tender wing of Joy, beautiful divine spark, daughter of Elysium.* Like every other hymn, the "Ode to Joy" contains a utilitarian transparency and an almost journalistic comprehensibility. It does not ask for esoteric interpretations. If it were not true, the cry *All men will become brothers* could represent an announcement of apocalypse; in other words a historical turning point, an annunciation of a time in which every new war, in the most direct meaning of the term, would represent a *fratricide.* Nevertheless, I will not treat biblical parables about brothers here, nor will I talk about royal battles for thrones and inheritance. What interests me is a story about two people whose works are paradigms of two opposed worldviews—of two contemporaries who, I first thought, merely shared a last name, which already seemed a sufficiently aphoristic paradox to me, but who turned out to be brothers. If a story about a pragmatic older brother is a cliché and a commonplace then this is its archetype. For the elder of the brothers is the founding father of the philosophical school of pragmatism. The maladjusted impracticality of the younger brother is not represented here in its deceitful and false aspect—in a perfectly adjusted and practical preaching of maladjustment and impracticality. A primordial consistency in one's own worldview is the same whether in life or in work. The younger brother's life, as well as his numerous *stories about life,* is more an image of life than a stance regarding it. Images of life—is it necessary to add?—completely contrary to the older brother's stance about what life should be like. Stories about completely different brothers owe part of their eternal contemporaneity to the fact that they are the very best refutation of all psychological hypotheses about character formation. Because there are no genes that resemble each other more closely than brothers' genes, and because both their upbringing and their surroundings are equally similar, all behaviorist theories and all theories of inheritance become inadequate. There are, of course, cases in which *generation gap* and global context tip the balance and prevail, defeating the microclimate of the family, but that happens only if there is a significant age difference. In this particular example, that difference is the slightest possible (if we exclude twins, of course)—about a year (more precisely, one year, three months, and four days). The equalization of upbringing and surroundings here is also brought to perfection, existing almost as a programmatic duty. For those who do not favor symbolist mysteriousness and camouflage, I will reveal the brothers' identity. They are William and Henry James.

The name of the brothers' father was the same as that of the younger brother, Henry. He, too, was not just anyone. Therefore all the better encyclopedias have two entries under the name Henry James. Henry James Senior was a renowned philosopher and theologian of his time. From the standpoint of the medieval concept *Ancilla theologiae,* this would mean that he was both master and slave in the same shape and form. However, there is one word that is usually used to characterize the man, a word that connects these two somewhat incompatible qualifications, a word that, just like the famous sentential definition of surrealist poetics, connects the seemingly incompatible: a Swedenborgian. William and Henry's father was an ardent follower of Emmanuel Swedenborg's teachings—the teachings of a man who, contrary to the Bible (*Blessed are the poor in spirit: for theirs is the kingdom of heaven*), used to preach that the soul in order to elevate itself first has to acquire intellect. He was a follower of the creator of the well-known maxim that best incorporates the essential doctrine of such intellectualized Christianity: *A fool will never set foot in heaven regardless of how saintly he is.* Therefore it is no surprise that his sons' education was the most sacred duty to this particular father. William and Henry got their elementary education in New York, in school, as well as in their own home. It is not difficult to imagine what lies beneath the worn-out phrase that reoccurs continually in the one-dimensional short biographies of the James brothers attached to their books, *a remarkably cosmopolitan education.* Piano chords blend with children's fidgeting in French pronunciation, trembling affectations of a violin become an overture to a loud recitation of strict and concise Latin proverbs, the mathematical logic of chess has its seamy side in the foggy canon of German grammar, the melody of poetry in their mother tongue soaks dry historic narratives with reality. There is no need to fall into anachronism here and consider this a kind of equivalent of today's caricatured and snobbish *sentimental education* with a tennis racket, solo scores, foreign language textbooks, and ballet shoes in which children are used as parents' status symbols, as if they were an automobile or jewelry. The education of the James brothers was inspired by their father's inner imperative, not by some kind of fashion-consciousness. Therefore the numerous moves of the James family (the transversal is Geneva–Paris–Boulogne–Bonn) should neither be considered tourist journeys nor migrations in search of a better living. These were simply the locations of the schools that

William and Henry attended and places where they visited museums and galleries as well as theaters. In those days visits to theaters were not considered acts of education and could have been seen as signs of their father's goodwill and indulgence. As an example of Henry Senior's progressiveness, James family biographers also mention the fact that he, even during dinner, while his sons were still little children, discussed all possible topics with them, treating them as his equals. And sometimes guests happened to be present at family dinners. A mention of their names almost resembles the counting of gods on some imaginary Anglo-American Olympus: Thoreau, Emerson, Hawthorne, Carlyle, Tennyson, John Stuart Mill. That was the milieu in which the brothers grew up. The merciless facticity of history once again does not allow for anachronism and therefore it is impossible to imagine different variants of the brothers' education—variants that would take into account their individual particularities and their individual choice of the subjects of their studies. Both brothers were subjected to the same educational canon. But, unfortunately, since the Renaissance institutionalized versatility dies after one turns eighteen. Expertise replaces broadness; specialization stands for roundness. A cynical contemporary of William's used to say that expertise was the knowledge of more and more details about a smaller and smaller scope of things, so a perfect expert was one who knew everything about nothing. Expertise is acquired through education at a university—that institution with an ironic name. At the age of eleven, William starts studying chemistry at Harvard. It needs to be stressed that a year earlier William entertained the thought of becoming a painter (the adolescent crisis of an older brother!), but, after spending six months serving under the apprenticeship of the painter Hunt, he quit, believing he lacked talent. The following year, the younger brother would enroll at university as well. He would, also at Harvard, commence studying law; nevertheless, his studying would end similarly to William's painting: he would quit after a year.

So, Henry left university once and for all—that institution that would adopt his brother for his entire life. It is here that the biographies of the James brothers begin to blend with the history of philosophy and psychology on the one hand, and that of literature on the other, so this story will not detail the unique chronology that, after all, is accessible to everyone. It will focus solemnly on the facts that impeccably, like some unknown star, situate their destiny in the eternal constellation of two brothers in conflict.

While William devotedly works toward obtaining a degree (to tell the truth, he, too, left his studies but only to start other ones; instead of chemistry he chose medicine), Henry publishes his essays, reviews, and first short stories in periodicals. His father perhaps regrets not having named his older son after him. When he asks William to exert his influence on his brother, hoping that the latter would return to the university, he answers smilingly, *Am I my brother's keeper?* During his studies, William often travels. His expedition into the Amazon is a part of a university project that deals with natural history, while during his stay in Europe, in France and Holland, William begins to show an interest in psychology. At the same time, in New England, Henry is interested in social expeditions, frequenting various receptions and salons where he explores the natural history of certain human characters, while his interest in psychology limits itself to recording the effects that different personalities have on the lives of their bearers. In 1869 William successfully completes his studies in medicine and takes his diploma, while Henry travels to Europe convinced that America exercises brutality against any artistic talent. That was the year William celebrated his twenty-seventh birthday, an age that already requires a clearly drawn sketch of a life's journey. It is almost a rule that unfortunate rockers die at that age, most often in a suicidal way. This is because, to modern profane symbolism, the age of twenty-seven carries all of the polysemous emblematics that the Kabbalistic and Christian traditions used to ascribe to the age of thirty-three. Therefore, the six years between the two symbolic birthday-based turning points (of course for those who overcome the *black point* of twenty-seven, that new age Scylla and Charybdis) represent a time of empirical interplay, life's interlude. Before he reached Christ's age William would overcome a psychological crisis triggered by his poor health and become an instructor of anatomy and physiology at Harvard. The famous thirty-third birthday would find him as the very first psychology instructor in the United States. At that time, Henry travels through Europe on the line London–Paris–Rome—a route that could today immediately be associated with diplomacy. Henry would publish his first novel, and that same year he would decide to make Paris his home. There, he would add to the virtual gallery of renowned contemporaries with whom he had associated since his childhood—the figures of Flaubert and Turgenev. But Henry would endure Paris only for a year; after November he would float with the spring tides. He too would meet his thirty-third birthday somewhat calmly, living in London *for good.* It was in that year that his father and namesake would, like the Old Testament Jehovah, announce to his older son that he had met his spouse-to-be. After a brief and useless obstinacy and a two-year courtship William would actually marry the teacher and pianist, Alice Howe Gibbens, seven years his junior. She would give birth to his five children, the first son after only a year of marriage. William would name his first child Henry. Thus he would have three Henrys as his closest male relatives, his father, his brother, and his son, like in a variation of English history or Shakespeare. Brother Henry would never marry. The most important and best known of all his relations with women would be his youthful enchantment with his relative, Minny Temple, who would die in the prime of her life, and a platonic relationship with the author Constance Fenimore Woolson, which would end in a first-class decadent way—with her suicide in Venice. William's mature age—the next twenty years—would bring advances in his university career following a familiar pattern. The impeccable older brother's ability to predict the movements of the *global spirit* is evident from the fact that he was the first American to pay attention to the work of the Viennese doctor Sigmund Freud. During the twenty years that brought William a full professorship in psychology and philosophy, Henry lived in London, writing books and looking for a pattern in the carpet. At the end of the last decade of the nineteenth century Henry would leave London to settle down in a rustic house in the country, in Sussex. William's old age consisted of gaining titles and degrees, publishing books and works of various provenance, cycles of lectures, and family joy with his children. Henry lives the life of a nun, dedicated solemnly to his books: Flaubert's successor, and the progenitor of Joyce, a follower of Mallarmé's famous motto. In the year 1910 William dies at the age of sixty-eight. Henry would die six years later, after officially becoming a subject of the British Crown, renouncing his American citizenship in protest against America's lack of involvement in World War I. That particularly appropriate conversion, it appears, made him eligible for an official acknowledgment, for the Order of Merit. However, probably due to irony, after his death America would get involved in World War I after all.

It is a fact that the spirit works more weakly than symbols. The accumulation of data is often an act of creating *maya's veil,* a veil that covers both core and essence. Therefore comparing the most concise textbook digest of William's philosophy to Henry's autopoetic meditations regarding the novel, included in a selection of the best novels in the world literary tradition along with the marginalia about their creators, perhaps could summarize everything their lives hide behind their prolixity, since their work truly was their lives' essence. A high-school *History of Philosophy* summarizes William James's doctrine in these words: *Metaphysical solutions, according to James, depend on the psychic constitution of a person; therefore an emotional, tender personality would treat appearances differently than a strong and resolute one. If one approaches the truth from a pragmatic standpoint, one finds the most reliable set of criteria. James thinks that everything we have to believe in is truthful, and we believe in everything that is best for us to believe in. If one summarizes these two claims, it becomes clear that we find truthful everything that is best for us to believe in.* How profoundly different from this manifesto of cheap pragmatism are Henry James's ideas about the novel as *the fruit of a boundless sensibility, some kind of an enormous spiderweb whose most tender silky threads are stretched in the space of consciousness and, as such, are capable of keeping even the smallest particle they come across on its surface.* The same sources summarize and report on the destiny of the brothers' opus: *Due to his extraordinary style, and (and this is probably more important) to the fact that his philosophy perfectly fits the social being of the American citizen to whom pragmatism is much better suited than any other kind of philosophical speculation, the popularity of William James is great, while his influence has surpassed the borders of America.* The younger brother earned the following remark: *In his desire to follow and fix each and every smallest possible psychological and ethical nuance, Henry James, however, often recognizes no borders. His long, convoluted, idiosyncratic meandering sentences require absolute concentration and enormous attention that only the smallest circle of his aficionados can completely provide.*

Perhaps, at first sight, the cruelty of the biblical forefathers and the Levantine bloodthirsty slyness of the Ottomans do not resemble too closely the cultivated lives of these two noble American men. However, the ancient essence does not vanish nor weaken in the course of civilization's progress. Cosmetic interventions only enable various manifestations of difference and intolerance. Criminal law, not morals and ethics, stops murderers. To God, all stories about two brothers represent nothing but the same side of a coin. To people, too. Because, in spite of Henry's posthumous glory, only a few people will find it reasonable to compare a happy father of five, a respectable professor, and a scholar to an ascetic weirdo prone to bizarre and somewhat incestuous fixations. This is a story of Cain and Abel (although Abel might have survived Cain), these are, after all, Bajazit and Džem-sultan.

Translated from the Bosnian by Nikola Petković and Andrew Wachtel

■ □ ■ □ ■

FIAT IUSTITIA

The white moonlight was cold and clear,
Like the justice we dream of but don't find.

Raymond Chandler

Melting in a barrel, like salt,
a star, and the icy water is ever blacker,
death cleaner, pain more bitter,
And the earth is terrible and just.

Osip Mandelstam

I

Archetypically, justice is blind, like love or a poet. But there is often another attribute connected to justice, one that does not belong to justice's blind relatives—slowness. Love and justice are difficult to reconcile anyway. From a metaphysical point of view, love is often unjust in the sense of active and passive mismatching, or due to the fact that one who loves is often not loved and vice versa. Even in the banal, everyday understanding of love and justice, they are irreconcilable: in court it is permissible to refuse to testify against a spouse. It is much less thankless to link poets and justice and to get, as a result, poetic justice, which is difficult to define abstractly. I will try to do it through two examples. Borges, as the paradigm of poetry of the modern era, was necessarily blind like the leading poets of earlier epochs—Homer and Milton. The founder of Rome was Romulus, the first Roman emperor was Augustus, and the last emperor of Rome was Romulus Augustus. Some would call that poetic justice, and others irony.

2

It is precisely ancient Rome that had immeasurable significance for the concept of justice in both of the aforementioned senses. As far as the everyday aspect goes, it is enough to mention that Roman law is a required subject even today at law schools all over the world, *iuris prudentes* from that time—specialists in legal advice and the profession of lawyer—to which these were predecessors—were created precisely in ancient Rome. The first famous lawyer was Cicero. There is a well-known case of a Greek poet, whose status as a Roman citizen was in question, and for whom Cicero, through a speech in honor of his poetic artfulness, won him—as we would say today—citizenship. Even the emperor Augustus himself appeared once as a lawyer at the request of a soldier. The soldier, in fact, asked the emperor to represent him in court. The emperor promised to send a deputy to act in his name, to which the soldier retorted that he had not sent a deputy to replace him in the battle of Actium but had instead fought there himself. The embarrassed emperor then appeared after all. The soldier appealed to the emperor's sense of justice, that fundamental justice that often has nothing in common with laws and customs. The most obvious plea for this kind of justice is the Roman proverb: *Fiat iustitia, pereat mundus*—Let there be justice, even if the world is destroyed.

3

According to this proverb the world is obviously not built on a foundation of justice. Otherwise, why would the world have to be destroyed for justice to prevail? A Sufi proverb confirms this as well: *As thirst proves the existence of water, so does thirst for justice prove the existence of justice.* For some interpreters of this saying this is proof of the existence of another world, because, according to them, there is no justice in this one. But because of the mere existence of even this world of ours, it is necessary, according to ancient thought, for a certain amount of justice to exist. Without it the world could not exist.

4

The most wonderful manifestation of this view is the Jewish legend about the thirty-six just men. According to it, at every moment in the world there are thirty-six just men who make the existence of the world possible. Usually they are ordinary, unexceptional men, by necessity completely unaware of their mission. A just man never knows he is a just man, just as no one else knows it other than God. Also, the just men do not know one another and according to tradition at the moment when one just man dies, somewhere in the world another one is born. Without this the world would be destroyed.

5

Why exactly thirty-six just men? Thirty-six is a fine number in the numerical and Kabbalistic sense. This is not to say that its immediate predecessors are not fine (thirty-three as Adam's and Christ's age, thirty-four as the sum of the diagonals of the famous magic square on Dürer's engraving *Melancholia I,* thirty-five as the Pythagorean harmony), but the number thirty-six conquers them all. Of the nine single-digit numbers, thirty-six is divisible by six (one, two, three, four, six, and nine) and at the same time it is six squared. I will remain silent about numerous other mystical possibilities connected with this number, mentioning only the fact that it unites the number three and the number twelve, which, when multiplied, make it—three, the holy number of Christianity, and twelve, the holy number of Judaism.

6

Judaism is based on law, and Christianity on love or feeling. In that sense they are close to that dual apprehension of justice—everyday and foundational. By themselves these two kinds of justice are not worth a lot, but true justice is formed by their fusion or multiplication, when the number thirty-six—like in some algebraic version of Wilkins's analytical language—becomes a synonym for justice.

7

Wilkins based his analytical language—according to Borges—on Descartes' idea that it would be possible to make a perfect language in which every number would stand for one concept. It would be a modern and more complicated version of ancient hieroglyphs, but lacking pictorial elements. In such a language the number thirty-six would mark the notion of justice.

8

Alberto is thirty-six years old. He is a just man. I know it and there is nothing strange about it. If God as the creator of the world knows who the just men in his world are, so do I, as a creator of my own world, know who is a just man in it. Alberto teaches philology. I mention this fact although it is not particularly important, because being a just man is not based on one's profession. Still, people of just-man constitution could hardly occupy certain professions, just as they share the attribute of patient tranquility.

9

Borges wrote a poem that beautifully describes one imagined generation of just men, although it seems that the fourth and seventh lines contradict the final one:

THE JUST

A man who cultivates his garden, as Voltaire wished.
He who is grateful for the existence of music.
He who takes pleasure in tracing an etymology.
Two workmen playing, in a café in the South, a silent game of chess.
The potter, contemplating a color and a form.
The typographer who sets this page well though it may not please him.
A woman and a man, who read the last tercets of a certain canto.
He who strokes a sleeping animal.
He who justifies, or wishes to, a wrong done him.
He who is grateful for the existence of Stevenson.
He who prefers others to be right.
These people, unaware, are saving the world.[1]

10

So then, on what basis can a person be a just man, if not on that of his profession? It seems that the logical answer is—on birth. But does a person become a just man by a momentary choice or by predestination? Is it known in advance who will be a just man, is there already a list of all past, present, and future just men in a heavenly register, or is it that upon the death of one just man the most suitable of all the children born at that moment is chosen to bear the burden of saving the world? I do not know the answer to this question and I do not know whether anyone else has already been looking for it, but this question leads to another more important and complicated one: can a just man cease to be a just man? Could he lose his title and honor by some act? If that were to happen it is difficult to imagine that some other person could suddenly become a just man, and a new child–just man could not be born since the (already former) just man has still not died. In that case, the world would, it seems, be destroyed.

11

But for a just man to do something inappropriate, something that would take away his status of just man, he would have to be forced into it in some way. If he committed some kind of villainy all of a sudden that would mean that he had never really been a just man. It would have to be a temptation such that the human (for even just men are human) would overshadow the cosmic, and on the border of which, like a watermark on a bill, there would be an inscription visible in light etched in gothic script: *Fiat iustitia, pereat mundus.*

12

Alberto is breaking down. In last thirty-six months he has gone gray, it seems to him exactly because of the torments of a dilemma. Alberto, in fact, wants to kill Daniel. He feels that Daniel deserves to die. Personal reasons are the cause. Daniel killed a few people close to Alberto. Alberto knows that for sure, and Daniel does not know that Alberto knows. The two of them do not know each other. Let's also say that it would be difficult (actually, impossible) to accuse Daniel through a legal juridical process. The other details are not important.

13

Jewish and Christian views on revenge as an instrument of justice differ diametrically. The Old Testament says: *An eye for an eye,* while in the New Testament God says: *Vengeance is mine and I will repay.* In Christianity revenge is—thus—very unpopular and represents, so to speak, a theft of booty from God's claws, which does not seem like a smart thing to do. But by accepting revenge and supposing the equality between crime and punishment we come to a problem of a quantitative nature.

14

When in the continuation of that *eye for an eye* it says *a tooth for a tooth, a life for a life, a death for a death,* that is not as simple as it may seem at first glance. In fact, if someone is killed he obviously cannot kill his killer. Someone else has to do it for him. It would be best if the revenge taker were someone not of this world, but that the revenge be carried out in this world. But most often it does not happen this way (*dixit Ecclesiastes: but on Earth there is void and a just man meets the same destiny as a vicious one, and the vicious meet the destiny of the just*). And so a relative or a friend of the victim kills the killer. And although he is only paying back a debt, the blood remains on him as it does on the tray of a scales for weighing meat.

15

The scales are a symbol of justice because the basis of justice should be equality. But equality is first and foremost a mathematical category, and mathematics is abstract and thus distant from real life. In physics or chemistry there are units at least, and thirty-six amperes is not the same as thirty-six coulombs, just as thirty-six atoms of hydrogen is not the same as thirty-six atoms of helium. But in mathematics thirty-six is the same as thirty-six and that's that. Thirty-six just men or thirty-six villains, it makes no difference. The positive annihilates the negative.

16

Even the uniqueness of the number thirty-six does not derive from mathematics. In mathematics there are no equal numbers (in the sense of size), all numbers are different, but still they are all the same. Mathematics is in that sense just, but only because it is abstract. Does this mean that justice is merely an abstraction or smoke, an incubus, only the outermost layer of maya's thick veil, the trace of a barren human desire just as a lithograph is the imprint of an original plate?

17

That art and mathematics are not particularly related and that people with an inclination toward both of these areas of *weltgeist* are rare is already something of a commonplace. The alleged question *Qu'est-ce que cela prouve?* asked by a certain mathematician after reading Racine's *Iphigenia* has become paradigmatic. Other than music, which has been compared to mathematics from the days of Pythagoras's school all the way to Leibnitz's famous mot: *Musica est exercitum arithmeticae occultum nescientis se numerare animi,* the only exception to this view is visual art at least to some degree. Here I have in mind primarily the link between geometry and some tendencies in modern painting (like cubism), and especially the link between geometry and graphic art, whose fusion gave birth to cartography and Escher. In order for a graphic work to be art, the number of imprints of an original plate has to be limited (according to some, the limit is exactly thirty-six).

18

In a Borges sonnet, too, we find a link between visual art and mathematics. All one needs to do is to change the meaning a little bit (instead of one noun and one adjective put their opposites), and his poem could describe the feelings of a person who desires revenge:

IN LOVE

Months, roses, old instruments,
Ivory, a lamp, Dürer's line,
Nine numbers with zero, different letters,
I have to give the impression that there are these things.
I have to pretend of late that there were
Persepolis and Rome, claim that
Just a grain of sand can change the destiny of a fort,
That centuries destroyed.
I have to pretend that heavy weapons

Create an epic and that heavy seas
Gnaw at the earth's foundation. I have to claim
That others exist too, which is false.
Only you exist. You, my whole happiness
And anguish, purer and greater than anything.

19

Alberto is sitting in a bar next to a window in one of those modish cafés that are named after artists and on whose walls hang reproductions of their famous works. While the music drowns out the street noise passing by the bar, Alberto is looking at a reproduction of Dürer's engraving *Ritter, tod und teufel—Knight, Death, and the Devil.* The hourglass in the devil's hand is turning into a scales for Alberto.

20

This engraving with its overall bluish background seems to recall that nonexistence that Novalis considered dark bluish. The observer usually identifies himself with the knight here, but the knight's look, with a shadow of disdain, is not proof that the scales are tipped in his favor. The scales should perhaps judge how the knight is resisting temptation, and perhaps they are there only as a sign that the knight arrived where he should have.

21

This engraving is the only painting to which Borges dedicated a poem. That poem (in fact, two poems) was created in a period when blindness had already become Borges's old companion:

TWO VERSIONS OF KNIGHT, DEATH, AND THE DEVIL

I

Under the unreal helmet the severe
Profile is cruel like the cruel sword
Waiting, poised. Through the stripped forest
Rides the horseman unperturbed.
Clumsily, furtively, the obscene mob
Closes in on him: the Devil with servile
Eyes, the labyrinthine reptiles

And the ashen old man with the hourglass.
Iron rider, whoever looks at you
Knows that in you neither the lie
Nor pale fear dwells. Your hard fate
Is to command and offend. You are brave
And you are certainly not unworthy,
German, of the Devil and of Death.

II

There are two roads. That of the man
Of iron and arrogance, who rides,
Firm in his faith, through the doubtful woods
Of the world, between the taunts and the rigid
Dance of the Devil with Death,
And the other, the short one, mine. In what vanished
Long-ago night or morning did my eyes
Discover the fantastic epic,
The enduring dream of Dürer,
The hero and the mob with all its shadows
Searching me out, and catching me in ambush?
It is me, and not the paladin, whom the hoary
Old man crowned with sinuous snakes
Is warning. The future's water clock
Measures my time, not his eternal now.
I am the one who will be ashes and darkness;
I, who set out later, will have reached
My mortal destination; you, who do not exist,
You, rider of the raised sword
And the rigid woods, your pace
Will keep on going as long as there are men.
Composed, imaginary, eternal.[2]

22

Alberto is looking through the window now. He is waiting for Daniel. He arranged to meet him here on some pretext. He intends to kill him. He has figured out a plan for the perfect crime, the perfect revenge: he will kill Daniel and tell him why he is killing him so that he will perceive his death as an implacable punishment and not just an accident, a product of caprice and coincidence. According to his plan there is no possibility that anyone could suspect him, that he could eventually be held responsible. After a lot of thinking internally, he has equated revenge with justice and any other illumination or consideration of that matter is unnecessary for him. But the particular details of the plan do not interest us here. If Alberto carries out his plan there will be no foundation for the further existence of the world.

23

The world will come to an end. The only reason why it can still continue to exist is that the world does exist. How weak this reason is in comparison with all those that suggest the opposite, especially with this: what is the world to do from now on under the heavenly vault? Thus wrote Baudelaire, from whose perspective there were no just men. And truly there would be nothing to object to in this paragraph were it not for the existence of that minimal dose of meaning incarnated in the thirty-six just men, although his principal reason does not seem particularly convincing. Because if not knowing what to do from now on would mean the end, the vast majority of people would immediately come to an end. But melancholic men have always asked *what to do* questions, especially under the influence of hashish when they seem unavoidable and imperative like a divine commandment.

24

In Paris Baudelaire was a member of *a hashish club*. Smoking hashish, a person loses the sense of time, and, for the first time, poetic experience acquires the second attribute of justice—the slowness of concepts, like objects to a drunk, double, and then it seems that love separates from movements during copulation just as justice distances itself from the meaning of judicial procedure.

25

At the time of the trial of *The Flowers of Evil* Baudelaire is thirty-six. That age in the life of poets has always been significant, just as the age of twenty-seven is significant for rockers. (Perhaps it would be interesting to consider if it is an accident that the descent from a poet to a rocker expresses itself in this way, in exactly a period of nine years, nine years that represent a quarter of thirty-six.) Burns and Byron die at thirty-six, and at that age Dante's foot *enters the dark forest* (another connection between a poet and thirty-six—the thirty-sixth sura of *The Koran* talks about poets). Baudelaire is sitting in the seat of the accused, he is despondent, *great weariness seized his consciousness.* He was smoking hashish and—as we would say today—he is *down.* Probably he thinks: *they are trying me as if I were an assassin.*

26

Assassino, assassino—Alberto feverishly repeats to himself. It is not easy for a person to think like this, and for a just man it is even harder. But, while the words and sounds of one of those rock-and-roll songs that glorify drunkenness and drugs in ambiguous expressions blare from speakers affixed to those places where two walls and the ceiling come together, his face lights up for a moment. He must have remembered grass, then hashish, then the Old Man of the Mountain, and then an Ismaili sect. (Here is another proof that Alberto is a just man—*with pleasure he traced etymology.*)

27

The French, Italian, and Spanish words for a murderer (*assassin, assassino, asesino*) come from a name of a radical Ismaili sect—the assassins (or hashashins—those who eat hashish). The founder of this sect, Hasan-i Sabbah (known in Europe as the Old Man of the Mountain) wrote: *And Kairos appeared, holding in his hand a scepter that signifies royal dignity, and he gave it to the first created god, who took it and pronounced: "Your secret name will consist of thirty-six letters."*

28

A name hides the secret of a being, the core of the thing itself. And the God of the Old Testament has a secret name—YHWH (because of that the ancient Hebrews revered a magic square made of the numbers from one to nine which in each row, column, and diagonal has a sum of fifteen; the letters of their alphabet had numerical values, and the sum of the letters Y and H, the first two letters of God's name, was exactly fifteen), and Moses introduced himself as *ehje aser ehje*—I-that-am. In ancient Egypt people had two names: a small name that everyone knew, and a large, true, secret name. And Rome, at the time of Republic, had a secret name that was discovered by Quintus Valerian Soran, a blasphemy for which he was punished by death, and soon Rome ceased to exist as a Republic. Perhaps justice as well really exists, but it is hiding under a false name like some ruler who travels incognito and the only thing that could reveal him is the discreet royal seal on his ring.

29

Besides its rings, Saturn has nine satellites. One of them is Times, named after the Greek goddess of justice. This Latin alphabet transcription of the name of the ancient Greek goddess in today's English-dominated and journalistic epoch necessarily recalls an association with time, an association furthered by the mention of Saturn—the Roman god of time.

30

And thus time travels through the universe, and justice circles around it and travels together with it. The attracting force of time keeps justice at a set distance forever. But from this perspective Saturn and Times are too similar to mathematics, too abstract, and therefore it would be better to use an analogy to bring our allegory closer to the place of action. Earth would become time, and the moon—justice.

31

Justice lights the darkness sparingly and is visible only in darkness. Its shape seems to change, but justice is always the same. One of its sides—always the same one—is forever invisible. When seen from a distance the external appearance of justice is like a human face of indeterminate expression that can shift in a moment from charitable to cruel, like an optical illusion with faces and a vase. Sometimes it is invisible, and sometimes it shines like a silver-plated sun. At times it looks like a sickle or a sword, and at times like a ducat. It is possible to predict when it will be eclipsed. It shines with a light that is not originally its own. It is eighty-one times lighter than time. To reach it *is a small step for a man, but a giant leap for mankind.*

32

The moon has surfaced on the sky although it is still daytime. Alberto nervously looks at his watch. Daniel is late. Alberto lights a cigarette, he measures time with the help of cigarettes.

He feverishly drinks the rest of his coffee and orders a cognac. Perhaps he does not know what he wants: should Daniel show up or not?

33

On the opposite sidewalk, Alberto sees Daniel. He is beautifully dressed, with a bag in his hand, and he is also looking nervously at his watch, it seems that he is hurrying somewhere (to his meeting with Alberto, his meeting with death), still he waits at the zebra crossing for the green light. Alberto's hands are shaking as he downs his cognac in one gulp. The cars have stopped, but Daniel still does not cross the street. He waits ten seconds in case some driver, who saw yellow light in the distance, were to sweep by irresponsibly. Then he slowly starts walking across the pedestrian crossing. But just then (through the red light) a black Fiat (Fabrica italiana automobili Torino) that had been quietly stopped till then starts moving violently and in the short distance accelerates tremendously and runs right over Daniel. It is obvious that he is dead. The Fiat has already disappeared from view.

34

Alberto was aghast. He had been ready to take revenge but he was not expecting to take any pleasure in it. But although this came to him almost as if he had ordered it, like getting a deuce when you have nineteen in blackjack, still it seemed unreal, a true deus ex machina. So how does it seem to the reader?

35

If God created the world, then maybe he could do some trivial thing to save it. Today a car is a completely suitable substitute for a burning bush, in this case an even more meaningful one. Because in the beginning there was the word, and if we believe the Bible, God created the universe with a word. According to the Vulgate, God's first word was Fiat, the verb in the sentence: *Fiat lux!*

36

Alberto has calmed down. He is sitting alone in the café because the waiters and the two or three remaining guests have walked out in front where they are waiting for the police, looking at the dead body, cursing, and marveling. Alberto walks out with a cigarette in his mouth, pays the waiter, and quickly goes away without waiting for the change. He wants to avoid interrogation and investigation. Perhaps he does not want to say that he saw the number thirty-six on the license plate of the black Fiat as well as one of those stickers on the rear window that motorcyclists often stick on the front of their bikes—a populist symbol of justice: a beautiful woman, blindfolded with scales in her hands. So he walks away quickly, and the wind plays with the lapels of his coat.

Translated from the Bosnian by Oleg Andrić and Andrew Wachtel

■ □ ■ □ ■

THE SECOND BOOK

> Thus there are two bookes from whence I coolect my Divinity; besides that written one of God, another of his servant Nature, that universall and publik Manuscript, that lies expans'd unto the eyes of all; those that never saw him in the first, have discovered him in the second.
>
> Sir Thomas Browne, *Religio Medici*

THE MASS OF MYSTIFICATIONS THAT SURROUNDED THE PERSONA OF Ian Tishri during his life grew rapidly and significantly after his death on December 27, 1990. What follows is merely the result of a desire to finally tell the truth, the truth that both the classical writers and Ian Tishri's beloved Schopenhauer took to be the only motive for their own writing. It should be said immediately that the responsibility for the large number of aforementioned untruths lies in the eternal human temptation to blacken a dead man in a low and undignified way, thereby attempting to deny his last wish that so perfectly and with almost terrifying consistency emanates from the course of his entire life. Ian Tishri, even at the moment of death, remained loyal to the ideal to which he had devoted his life. Here in a short and concise way, I will try to recount the facts about the life of Ian Tishri, a life in which loyalty and devotion to capricious and concrete readings of certain modern amphibolia[1] were the inseparable companions of an always restless and curious spirit.

Ian Tishri was born on May 1, 1922, in New York, as the first and only child in a strange and unusual marriage. The only thing that connected the families of his parents was wealth. It must have been that the red-haired goddess of irony was godmother to this fusion of the huge estate of the Jewish bankers Tishri and the fabulous estate of the Irish factory-owning Fitzpatricks. And the only heir to this inexhaustible Semitic-Celtic treasury would be born on the proletarian holiday. It is unknown where, when, or how David Tishri and Beatrice Fitzpatrick *started to fancy each other,* but it is totally clear that their sullen and unhealthy passion did not belong to the snobby bloodless beds of deliberation and calculation. And although both families had fantasized about the fusion of their own estate with another equally valuable one, this was not the fusion they had desired. Nevertheless, the young spouses—despite their lyrical ostentation and their refusal to make economic judgments about love—created an empire as a by-product of their love. Ian Tishri would come onto the world's stage as a prince.

Neither David nor Beatrice was an only child, but the disheveled mane of all-mighty chance would make them the legatees of two rivers of treasure, rivers that many generations of their predecessors had filled up with a Tigris and Euphrates of sweat, rivers that would merge in Ian into a Shatt al Arab. David's brother Abraham would die at age seventeen of tuberculosis, like Michael Furey, while Beatrice's brother James, the only male Fitzpatrick, like some Kabbalist, would turn his back on the world, and after completing theological studies would be ordained and return to his historical homeland to study the Bible in some isolated monastery.

A mélange of certain fragments from Schopenhauer's and Freud's systems could perhaps best interpret the progress of David's and Beatrice's marriage. After the *instinct of the species* had been satisfied, David found a new *investment of libido* in *business.* Passion turned into an average and prosaic marriage. Paraphrasing Freud, I also touched Ian's tribe on his father's side; in order not to shortchange the maternal component of his bloodline, I will mention one Irishman who, on the occasion of the collapse of his as well as any other love, would say: *to love oneself is the only true romance.* But, like the world itself, love ends not with a bang, but with a whimper. And in the context of everyday life a whimper is more pleasant and closer to happiness than any kind of bang. Though it seems paradoxical, the Tishris' marriage was happy, because generally passion is not the foundation of a happy marriage. It is torment, fervor, *passion;* and a marital bed needs to be like an olive trunk planted in the soil, it needs to be made of such a tree, and to be immovable.

Ian Tishri had a happy childhood nicely spiced with that Kunderaesque metaphor about the melancholy of a child without a brother. Such a child plays with the world. A true game requires seriousness: in order to play with something, first we need to get to know and to unmask that something (whatever it is). That is why all the innumerable anecdotes about Ian's earliest childhood contain this moment of desire to learn about the things of this world. The theme and subject of all of these childhood happenings are not some exotic actions. In essence, they are an ordinary child's snivels characteristic of a young human. Because childhood is a period of metaphysical equality: a time in which poverty and wealth are equally shiny, a time of the short-lived triumph of learning over owning. Though, somewhat later, the desire to own can hardly be ignored. But this desire is generally motivated by lack. For Ian, ownership was something natural and he reached knowledge through play.

It is not my intention here to create a chronicle of the lives of the wealthy in New York in the thirties at the time of Ian's early youth and farewell to childhood. That ambience is close to the spirit of Fitzgerald's novels: the Jazz Age, beau monde, drinking parties, travels, soirees, splendor, and extravagance. And although both branches of Ian's ancestors belonged to the conservative edges of their community circles, he fell into a whirlwind of youth that did not pay attention to ancestors and ancestry and was interested only in money, be it aristocratic or new, Jewish-Catholic or WASP. David and Beatrice Tishri, spouses who were a product of a somewhat Blakean marriage of the Old and New Testaments, themselves knew the adolescent inclination to defy authority, just as they knew the parable of the prodigal son. So Ian's excesses were financed, and his behavior was not even the subject of his parents' criticism. With some inherent subtle sensitivity his parents knew and felt that the power of rebellion grows stronger if it is banned and that the shine in an adolescent's eyes, like the shine of a lightbulb, is most often powered by the energy created by damming the natural flow of a river or of life. And so Ian drank insatiably from the well of the world, but he became thirstier and thirstier. Because the water of this world is seawater and it does not quench thirst.

The sun of war shone upon the sea of Ian's life in his twentieth year. Water evaporated, disappeared: only sediment, essence, and salt remained. Ian voluntarily joined the military in a desire to exchange the snobbish spritzer of sweet life for true undiluted wine. His parents saw in this decision the unwanted fulfillment of their prophecy. Tired of laxity and weak will Ian was searching for toughness and discipline. Thirty-six days after his twenty-second birthday, on the renowned D-day, which in its numerical form contains an incomplete symbol of the devil, the devil's number, Ian stepped on European soil for the first time, leaving the imprints of his boots in the sand of Normandy's beaches. Those days he discovered that blood is salty, like seawater.

Precisely a year after the famous D-day he returned home. The war was as senseless as drinking parties. Everything had remained the same in New York. It seemed that everyone was still drinking the same cocktail they had started five years before. Ian was not able to orient himself at the parties of his former friends: he who does not get drunk on wine, throws up from spritzers. In the fall of the following year David and Beatrice both could have acted the role of Hamlet: *O my prophetic soul!* Ian Tishri enrolled in a university to study French and Italian. But he must have soon recognized that if anything is truly far from real knowledge and mastery in any field then it is sugary college melodramatics. Schopenhauer would later confirm that. He left the university and spent the following few months trying to fit into the mold that destiny had picked for him. But those twenty or so weeks, during which he worked with his father and for the first time interested himself in all those different deals that occurred under his family name, brought him the knowledge that a modern business empire is similar to a constitutional monarchy: an owner, like a king, is just a name. And money is in some sense like an atomic bomb: the requisite amount or critical mass makes quality from quantity, and then the reaction continues by itself. It is difficult to say if Ian had ever seriously thought of devoting himself to the conventional career of inheritor, but the fact is that during this *business* apprenticeship of his, he also showed an interested in a *marriage based on interest.* It is more probable these were just a series of unsuccessful attempts to find a taste of love in some standard and old-fashioned relationship, a taste he had searched for in vain in the fast life of his crazy youth. But it seems that for him the storm of romantic passion and the lee of the marriage bed were just two faces of the same cheap coin: copper covered in fake gold. Anyway, one day Ian peeled off the face of convention just as he had removed his uniform with the arrival of peace.

At the age of twenty-six Ian seemed to return to childhood. Only, the real things his small hands had reached for in childhood were replaced now with various abstract concepts. And who knows, perhaps his whole life could have been just a series of fruitless and cheap false exaltations lasting on average three days each, if one of his first interests had not been genealogy. Inquiring about his ancestors and relatives, he found out the name of his uncle for the first time. Because the family had never mentioned James Fitzpatrick. His search for God and his particular mysticism were considered by the Fitzpatrick family to be worse, more shameful, and more suspect than open atheism, though the family proudly declared itself Catholic. Ian's passion to meet his uncle was partially inspired by their great physical similarity. Because the only photograph that Beatrice Tishri had of her brother showed him at age twenty, and if his frock had been replaced by a uniform, the photo could with equal probability have been of Ian from his military days. But for almost thirty years there had been no word from James. In 1920 he had sailed for Ireland with the intention of immuring himself in some monastery.

On March 12, 1949, Ian Tishri boarded a ship sailing for Ireland. He went to look for his uncle. The whole adventure bore a certain primordial air, an odor of foggy essence, almost classical. Because Ian had been in permanent crisis, a crisis of meaning and identity, since puberty. In its very breadth, all the variety of his life, all the wealth of his experience hid cracks and fissures. He understood the search for his uncle as a particular initiation rite, as some mixture of a bar mitzvah and a sacrament in accordance with his background, as the twelve labors of Hercules or the quest for the Golden Fleece, as some kind of imprimatur, as an exam of maturity and worthiness, as a metaphysical graduation. He would tell his uncle his whole life, admit everything to him as he would to himself, he would empty in front of him all the gold of his own soul to the last lump as in an intimate diary, he would confess to him as to a brother, to a stranger, to an uncle, to a grave, to a priest in the end, and he would ask for an answer as if from the Pythian oracle, from stars, or from coffee grounds.

Everything that is possible occurs; only the possible occurs—thus says an apocryphal aphorism of Kafka's, which, unbidden, answers the implied question: *How was it possible for Ian to find his uncle?* Because, truly, accident and fate conspired and Ian found Father James, who was already well known in County Mayo, quite quickly. He lived and prayed in Ballintubber Abbey in Clare Morris. This abbey was founded in 1216 by Cathal Crobhdearg O'Connor, King of Connacht, and it is the oldest active abbey in Ireland. Throughout the district Father James had almost saintly status. This young American, and a priest besides, who in the early twenties had come to a place whose young men were looking longingly toward the West, had, by means of his arrival, insane from the local perspective, achieved his own portrait, a portrait that was seen in the eyes of his new neighbors to be tinged with that shade of gold with which the haloes of those possessed by divine madness are painted. And when on the wings of rumors, larger and more powerful than the wings of that specter that was hovering over the other part of Europe, came the news that he was Fitzpatrick's only son, *that* Fitzpatrick, the young man in Clare Morris almost became what a certain Francesco had once been in Assisi. This news helped young James, at first glance paradoxically, in his desire for peace and loneliness. Because his life, his lifestyle, suffused with reading and contemplation, became what was expected from him. In time, a compromise developed between him and the local parishioners whereby Father James took confession from one of them each month. And only in those moments did he break his vow of silence: he would advise the penitent, but his advice always consisted of one (only one) short sentence. Local legend assigned to Father James's advice the power of healing and the certainty of prophecy.

The antique flavor of Ian's adventure was still secreting the saliva of exaltation. When he arrived in Clare Morris, old adepts said: *Young stranger's a copy of Father James!* The wings of rumor were efficient again. In a few days everyone knew that Ian was Father James's nephew. The truth of this rumor and the lack of even the smallest insinuation that Ian could possibly be Father James's son (though his age was approximately equal to the interval between the present and that time when the young priest had arrived in Clare Morris) illustrate in the clearest and most obvious way the widespread popularity of Father James among the population. Because any infinitesimal doubt in Father James's holiness would have initiated an entire gothic novel about sin *in illo tempore* and escape from an unwanted marriage. For similarity in appearance between a father and son is more common and more visible than between an uncle and a nephew. But, in any case, this rumor helped Ian (just as the old rumor had helped his uncle) and the locals gave him the next scheduled audience with Father James.

The meeting between Ian Tishri and his uncle James Fitzpatrick, Father James, was extraordinary. Nor was confession to Father James an ordinary confession. That is why these confessions were not held in the regular decor of a confessional, that system of connected containers, where the priest cannot see the face of the penitent, and where sounds of confession and admonition pass through a small window in a wall while remorse and forgiveness are exchanged through the wall by osmosis and diffusion. Confession to Father James was ornamented by a more intimate iconography: the penitent and the father confessor would sit next to each other in the last pew and the quiet sounds of confession could have almost been taken for whispers at a school desk. If the believer looked in Father James's eyes, the look was returned, if he looked into the floor or ceiling, Father James would do the same. Ian looked his uncle in the eyes while telling him his whole life. No trace of sentiment could be seen on the face of Father James, although at that critical moment when he stared for the first time at the still silent Ian, who was already swallowing him with his eyes, he must have recalled the legend of the magic mirror in which one sees a reflection of one's own youth, or Wells's time machine.

Father, I was born as a prince. No, I am not an aristocrat or a prince from some obscure unhappy country. I am prince of a modern empire of gold bars and paper banknotes. I have never learned that mechanism by which the desires of ordinary people are created and aroused, that mechanism that, like a lottery, does not guarantee fulfillment. From conception all my desires had within them the certainty of fulfillment, just as in every birth there sprouts the seed of death. So from early childhood I have looked for distraction in idleness. And, idleness is, as someone has said, the mother of all sins. This was said, I believe, by some composer, himself perhaps a real idler, but, I think, nevertheless not inclined toward sin. Idleness without punishment is, perhaps, permitted only to great souls like those wise men about whom the Talmud says that their sin committed in the evening is already forgiven by morning because they repent sufficiently during the night. But idleness was my enemy. The fact that my childhood wishes were fulfilled without exception was not damaging in itself, but such a development at a time of my early youth began to show its fatal consequences. At that time, Father, I did almost all of those things that the church calls sins, all except those that are the worst. But even that did not bring satisfaction. I did it all out of inertia, out of idleness. Quickly I was sated by such a life, and I was sick and tired of myself. At just about that time the war started and I signed up for the military. The almost geometric neatness of the military, its almost astronomical discipline and evolutionary order and hierarchy, gave me, for a short period, a desired counterweight. But the commonplaces of military mythology are true only during peacetime training. War itself recalls mostly a party *at full tilt: through a foggy glass everything is a somnambular ramble, and the dominant odor is some kind of juicy, sticky stink—a perfect mixture of the aromas of all bodily extracts, from those produced every day to the somewhat more exotic fruits of ejaculation and vomit. Upon returning from the war I tried to begin university studies, but that sterile apotheosis of mediocrity disgusted me more than anything. After that I tried to behave normally or in such a way as the statistical ghost of an average man would behave if he were in my shoes. It did not work. After having given myself over to short and almost pharisaical fads of ecstasy over trivial things a few times I realized that I was nowhere. Here I am with you, Father. What should I do?*

Son, seek the truth in the Second Book.

On the return trip to New York Ian did not sleep well. Through the alabaster labyrinths of his insomnia one sentence echoed, the only one he would ever hear from his uncle, Father James: *Son, seek the truth in the Second Book.* The magnitude of the expectations with which he had departed on the trip fused with James's reputation as a prophet and saint, like the wealth of the Tishris and the Fitzpatricks. His uncle's words became a password, a prayer, a mantra, a proverb, a haiku, a behest, and a *petit phrase.* During one of those painful insomnias, he reached for the Bible that was on the nightstand in his cabin as it is on the nightstand of some hotel room or on the edge of the wooden balustrade that surrounds the witness stand in court. He opened the Holy Scriptures as if for the first time. He opened the book randomly, like that governor from some Dostoyevsky novel who would, whenever he found himself in a dilemma, open some book and give prophetic value to the first sentence on the page to which the book opened. Ian glanced at the randomly turned page. On top there was a title: the Second Book of Kings. Ian trembled feverishly while he searched for the table of contents. In the Bible itself there were three additional Second Books: the Second Book of Moses (or Exodus), the Second Book of Samuel, and the Second Book of Chronicles. Happy and flustered, Ian skipped Genesis and slowly began to read Exodus: *Now these are the names of the sons of Israel . . .*

Throughout the crossing Ian read biblical Second Books. But it seemed to him that he did not find the truth, that there was perhaps some part of the truth here, a fragment of the truth, but that the whole truth was not here. In the New Testament there are no Second Books, and so he could not have read Pilate's famous question, the only biblical sentence Nietzsche considered worth reading: *What is the truth?* But he knew what he had to do when he arrived home: there are more Second Books.

The most beautiful room in the Tishri's magnificent house was the library. But this library, like many similar ones, was more a quiet corner for *business* agreements than a place for reading. Nor had Ian ever explored the contents of the wide shelves that completely covered the walls, like some bas-relief wallpaper. Now he looked at the spines of all, precisely all the books, and he took down those without a title on the spine, looking for a title on the cover. He was searching for a Second Book. He found two: Emerson's essays *Second Series,* and Kipling's *The Second Jungle Book.*

Some of Emerson's thoughts elated him, but he did not find in them what he would consider the truth. Kipling reminded him of childhood, that heavenly period when Mowgli's naive and picturesque adventures can fill and satisfy a spirit with ordinary narrative without a need for deep questions and pathetic answers. But after he had read these books he put them on the nightstand in his own room on which there had been until then only the Bible, the Bible that was somewhat unusual because it contained four bookmarks marking Second Books. In this way Ian Tishri started the creation of his famous library.

But his first encounter with the Second Book revealed something very important to him. A Second Book need not stand by itself. A Second Book could be just part of a book. This was guaranteed by those four prime examples with which he started his exploration of Second Books, it was guaranteed by the most distinguished authority: the Bible. His search of the house library based on consultations of the content of the books and not only on reading their titles yielded a much richer catch. He started with the Second Book of Plato's *Republic,* which says that the state does not need poets, and continued with the Second Book of Locke's *Essay Concerning Human Understanding* (*all ideas arise from sensation or reflection*), and with the Second Book of Spinoza's *Ethics,* which considers the nature and origin of the soul. All these Second Books gave joy to the spirit, but Ian did not know whether that joy was a sign of the presence of truth. But at one moment Ian suspected that the essence of his uncle's secretive Pythian advice was not the term "the Second Book," but the term "the truth." He was rescued from this small crisis by one particular Second Book and Ian hoped that it was only an auger and indication of the fact that there exists somewhere another Second Book (a Second Book squared), a true Second Book that would answer all of his deepest questions, that would reveal the truth to him just as the Second Book of Augustine's *Soliloquies* had answered the petty doubts expressed by the question that tormented him in his short-lived crisis, a question that represented an individual variation of Pilate's dilemma: is there truth and does it make sense to search for it?

> A.: *I see a very plain and compendious order.*
> R.: *Let this then be the order, that you answer my questions cautiously and firmly.*
> A.: *I attend.*
> R.: *If this world shall always abide, is it true that this world is always to abide?*
> A.: *Who doubts that?*
> R.: *What if it shall not abide? Is it not then true that the world is not to abide?*

A.: I dispute it not.

R.: How, when it shall have perished, if it is to perish, will it not then be true, that the world has perished? For as long as it is not true that the world has come to an end, it has not come to an end: it is therefore self-contradictory, that the world is ended and that it is not true that the world is ended.

A.: This too I grant.

R.: Furthermore, does it seem to you that anything can be true, and not be Truth?

A.: In no wise.

R.: There will therefore be Truth, even though the frame of things should pass away.

A.: I cannot deny it.

R.: What if Truth herself should perish? Will it not be true that Truth has perished?

A.: And even that who can deny?

R.: But that which is true cannot be, if Truth is not.

A.: I have just conceded this.

R.: In no wise therefore can Truth fail.

A.: Proceed as thou hast begun, for than this deduction nothing is truer.[2]

The advice of Saint Augustine was just an echo of James Fitzpatrick's advice. Ian continued as he had begun. Time passed, and Ian was still searching for the truth. He looked for it in each Second Book, and in Second Books. Two Second Books approached Ian's understanding of truth more closely than did the others: the Second Book of Schopenhauer's *The World as Will and Representation,* and the Second Book of Kierkegaard's *Either-Or.* But the problem of truth is a problem of finality. Ian could not be satisfied with just anything, because even when he discovered something somewhere that had the flavor of truth, he could not know whether this was just a tasteless imitation since he did not know the taste of real truth. His measure of truth was intellectual ecstasy, but even in a moment of great ecstasy it is impossible to know whether the ecstasy could be greater. The only way to check is to experience an even greater ecstasy. When something is accepted as the truth, it is hard to know if it is the closest thing to the truth that we have managed to reach until then or if it is finally the acme, the *final emancipation,* the real truth. The human heart is not an infallible angelic compass, the heart's North is not absolute.

Already by the mid-sixties Ian Tishri's famous library of Second Books contained an almost innumerable mass of tomes. It would be difficult here to employ the phrase usually used by snobs when they talk about the wealth of their mostly unread libraries: *it contains* so many *titles.* Because Ian Tishri's books both did and did not have the same or different titles. Only a small number of tomes had the words "The Second Book" in their titles, words to which there were usually added others (as in Kipling). Others contained a Second Book (as in Schopenhauer or Kierkegaard) or Second Books (as in the Bible). But two more things were common to all those books: all of them were in English and all of them were, in a certain sense, classics. Sometime toward the end of the sixties Ian Tishri decided that it was worth searching for truth in other languages and in unknown sources.

It was at about this time that the fame of Ian Tishri started to grow. Because susceptibility to gossip, unpleasant celebrity, and all kinds of rumors are one of those devastations that—as Pascal said—hurt us when we do not know that we should stay inside our own home. For with the exception of the most basic quotidian necessities, the only thing Ian Tishri spent his wealth on were Second Books. Because of Second Books he also learned foreign languages. In addition to French and Italian, which he had known earlier, he learned Spanish, Portuguese, German, Polish, and Russian. But besides procuring Second Books in different languages and those from the pens of varied anonymous writers, Ian's obsession with owning and reading every Second Book in order to finally find out the truth gave birth to another curiosity. As it happened, his many scouts for Second Books were flooding him with textbooks and anthologies consisting of two volumes and whose second volume, for practical reasons, had in its title "The Second Book," like a spy with a fake name. (Old writers knew well the difference between a volume and a book. It is impossible to mix up a second volume with, say, the Second Book of *The World as Will and Representation.* Division into two volumes is just a technical dichotomy, while a book is divided into multiple books in the same way that a symphony is divided into movements: based on content and harmony.) But it seems that Ian did not mind this quid pro quo. He read every Second Book for the first time with equal care. Because of that Tishri's library contains, among the others, *Second Poetry Book* by John Foster, and *Das Zweite Buch* by Otto Waalkes, and *The Second Book of Irish Myths and Legends* edited by Eoin Neeson, and *Vtoraja Kniga* by Osip Mandelstam, and *Druga Knjiga* by Muhamed Dženetić, and *Le Second Livre* by Charles Gerard, and *Alter Liber de Amores* by Ovidio, and *The Second Book of Modern Verse* edited by Jessie Belle Rittenhouse, and *Vtoraja Kniga* by Nikolay Zabolotsky, and *The Second Book* by James Woodstone.

Like many other passions, so this one kept growing with the passage of years, aging, and the approach of death. While in the seventies Second Books were arriving to Ian mostly from Europe, Australia, and the two Americas, the eighties brought the third world of Asia and Africa to the library of Second Books. Old age is not the ideal time for learning exotic languages. For that reason Ian Tishri employed young linguists to translate Second Books for him from Chinese, Arabic, Japanese, Hebrew, and various small languages of India and black Africa. Numerous young experts found starry moments of financial freedom working for Ian Tishri. One sociological study was written about the influence on enrollments in small philological departments at New York universities in the mid-eighties of the rumor that claimed there was a job flowing with milk and honey waiting at Ian Tishri's for every graduate of some faraway unknown language. So Ian Tishri spent his old age reading bound copies of unique translations of a variety of Second Books. A Mongolian literary magazine suggested that writers there should name their writings Second Books because that would guarantee them a translation into English.

In 1988 Ian Tishri, like Emperor Hadrian, began to realize the profile of his death. He had not found the truth and he knew and felt that he would never find it. Perhaps that is why his passion for reading Second Books slowly decreased, but that did not mean in any way that Second Books stopped coming to the house of Tishri, that postmodern Babylonian library. On the contrary, packages of books with colorful stamps continued to crowd the mailbox dedicated to Second Books, from where they were taken to Ian's house for unpacking and classification. On September 18, 1989, Ian Tishri wrote his famous will, somewhere also called the scandal of the century, by which he left his whole fortune to a council comprising his oldest and most loyal colleagues and suppliers, and this council was charged with spending the wealth entrusted to it exclusively for the acquisition of Second Books *and to turn the Tishris' house into a Library of Second Books,* which could be used gratis by all those interested but without removing the books. For that reason one room had to be turned into a reading room. The will was otherwise perfect in its strictness and level of detail, and it accounted for every possibility. Thus, for example, every member of the council had to delegate in his own will a person who would inherit his place, and Ian Tishri at just about that time bought the large house of his next-door neighbors, the Collinses, for an enormous amount of money (that was the first large sum of money not directly spent on Second Books) and in the will he arranged that this house was also to be used as a library if the Tishri house became too small for all the books.

Ian Tishri was not religious in a conventional sense. Perhaps one of the reasons was his ancestry, or the marriage of his parents, which did not give him a specific identity. But at the privileged moment of death, which differs from the analogous moment of birth by the presence of self-consciousness, Ian Tishri confessed to Samuel Wilson, his most loyal colleague and helper, a Slavist, and the first president of the council of the Library of Second Books. Perhaps he wanted to repeat the moment of confession to his uncle, Father James, the moment he considered to mark his own spiritual birth. And the term confession itself, it could be, reminded him of his ancestry and of one more strange similarity between the two tribes of his ancestors, of the Jewish-psychoanalytical reformation of the Catholic dogma of confession that was made by Sigmund Freud, that Viennese Luther.

It has now been more than forty years since I began reading and collecting Second Books. You know how everything started. If I return to that time when I waited for a ship to take me to the East, to Ireland, to find my uncle who was to tell me a reason for living, it is hard to believe my own luck. Soon I am going to the West and I know that my voyage to the East gave meaning to and saved my life. I was truly lucky.

Because to find a man from whom there had been neither trace nor voice for thirty-some years, and to find him as he was, that is divine luck. I often ask myself whether my uncle recognized me, but that is probably irrelevant. All of County Mayo *considers his advice as a formula for salvation. I have thought many times about this. How is it possible for someone to have such power? And many times I compared in my thoughts that abbey with the Temple of Delphi.* Ibis redibis numquam peribis in bello: you will go to war, get killed, not return *or* you will go to war, not get killed, return. *This prophecy for soldiers always comes true because in Latin the same phrase states and means both possible fates, so different; everything depends on whether that* numquam *(will not) is tied to* redibis *(return) or* peribis *(get killed). But my uncle's sentence was advice, not prophecy. For that reason it is not ambiguous. To me it looks like a testament from a folk story. In that story a father had three sons, and all three were slackers, lazybones, and idlers. He tells them on his deathbed that he is leaving them a huge treasure buried in the vineyard, but that even he himself does not know precisely where. The three start digging and of course they do not find anything because there is no treasure. But the well-aerated soil of the vineyard bears fruit like never before and the three realize that the true treasure is in work. And so I did not find the truth either, but I did find happiness and peace. Like Columbus I went looking for India, but found America. To myself I look like an alchemist. I did not find the philosopher's stone, but I accidentally discovered many other beautiful, important, and useful things. That is perhaps even better. Because, if that first* Second Book *had been the true one, or if some among the first ones were the true ones (as perhaps they were), what would have I done for the past forty years? But you are most interested, I'm sure, in my motives for making such a will. It is strange. Somewhere I read that all big things have a banal rationale. Then perhaps this testament of mine is a big thing. You know that for the last two years I have almost stopped reading Second Books. You certainly remember that for a while I read comic books. In one Italian comic the following story happens. A certain New York professor named Martin, a private detective as well, who deals with paranormal cases, meets some black hooligan who, after waking up from a coma into which he fell after being wounded in a robbery, is convinced that he is in fact a white girl named Annabel Lee. He even states the town he (or she) in fact comes from: it is an unknown small town in New England. The black man knows the humanities perfectly, too well for a vagabond, a homeless man, and a criminal without any schooling. He knows classical languages, and in Martin's presence he reads the* Iliad *aloud in the original. Martin becomes intrigued, thinks about some kind of reincarnation, and goes to the small New England town, but in the county records he discovers that no one with last name of Lee has ever lived there. After many complications the black man is killed, and the last scenes of the comic book occur in the small New England town where some man with the last name Lee has just moved in. He nervously paces the corridors of the hospital, because his wife is just about to give birth. In the hospital waiting room he notices a volume of poems by Edgar Allan Poe that was forgotten there, and at that instant he realizes that, if his child is a girl, he will give her the name Annabel so that she will be called Annabel Lee, just like in the poem. The black man, then, had truly been Annabel Lee, but her soul came into his body from the future, and not from the past. At that moment it hit me. Perhaps the true Second Book has not been written yet.*

Three days after this confession Ian Tishri died. The council carried out his last wish, continuing to collect Second Books from all over the world. But some distant relatives, in their immeasurable greed, are now trying to accuse the giant Ian Tishri of incompetence and to overturn his will. This chronicle is an attempt to defy the entire tide of slanders that many paid hacks are now producing for numerous publications. The only goal of this chronicle and the only purpose for its creation is the truth.

Translated from the Bosnian by Oleg Andrić and Andrew Wachtel

■ □ ■ □ ■

THE BRIDGE ON LAND

> But talking about Troy he is tempted to assign it the shape of Constantinople and to foresee the siege with which Mehmed, clever as Odysseus, will oppress it for many months.
>
> Italo Calvino

DURING THE SECOND YEAR OF HIS REIGN, AFTER AN UNINTERRUPTED victorious campaign, Sultan Mehmed arrived in the vicinity of Constantinople. Spring was beginning, *a cold and evil spring, which did not allow summer to shine.* At the beginning of April the whole Ottoman army camped before Constantinople, ready to erase from the map that final remaining part of Byzantium and *reliquie reliquiarum* of the famous Roman Empire. If we trust Virgil, this was the final act of the siege of Troy, because the besieged city was ruled by the last descendant of Aeneas, Constantine XI, who, not far from Anatolia and Schliemann's locations, was completing a circle that had been started by his forefather, Venus's son, who had carried his father on his shoulders and led his son by the hand as if in a symbolic vision of the paradigmatic genealogical tree of the imperial dynasty. Because every siege is the siege of Troy, and there is only one Troy. And it was truly the poet of shattered Byzantium, the modern Virgil, William Butler Yeats, who cried: *No Second Troy.* Even the emperor's name—Constantine—hinted at the end. For the Romans knew that because a circle starts and ends at the same point, the emperor who is the namesake of a city announces its beginning and its end. Constantine was the name of the Roman emperor responsible for the flag—a banner with a cross—under which his descendants were fighting, because on the night before a crucial battle he dreamed of a cross and the future inscription on packs of deluxe cigarettes: *In Hoc Signo Vinces.* But the emblems that were winning now were the sickle (lunar) and the star. In any case, the sickle, star, and cross, that holy trinity of symbolism, are in fact the only symbols. The sickle can be a lunar or a metal one; the stars can differ in the number of points; while the cross has three basic versions: one where the horizontal pole crosses the vertical pole in the middle (the Greek cross), then one where it crosses it halfway between the middle and the top (the Roman cross), and finally one where it crosses at the very top, in the shape of the letter "T" (the cross of Saint Anthony); this last version is also known as a hammer.

The hammer in Mehmed's ear, together with the anvil and stirrup, trembled continuously. The sultan was sitting in his tent trying to think despite of all kinds of noise around him: the neighing of horses; Ottoman soldiers yelling; the sounds of trumpets; the low clunk of a hammer hitting an anvil; the tinkle of swords, sabers, yatagans, daggers, helmets, armor, guns, spurs, and stirrups. The city was surrounded by a force that had never before been seen, but it was a city made for defense. Constantinople, unlike today's Istanbul, was not spread over two continents. It was primarily a European city. It was shaped like a triangle. One leg of this triangle faced the land, and that one was the most heavily fortified. At its foot the Turkish army was encamped; the second leg of the triangle looked toward the Bosporus, where seventy-two Ottoman galleys were sailing; the third leg of the triangle was also surrounded by water, by a bay, or the Golden Horn, which from the strait, notches deep into the European massif, but from the other side of the bay, along the whole length of the city walls there were stony and wooden barriers so that it was not possible to cross the walls, not even on the other shore on which several rows of hills were rising, among which there were narrow flat fields like hallways, while the entrance to the Golden Horn from the Bosporus was barred by chains. Roughly speaking, the residents of Constantinople had to defend themselves on one side from attacks by land, on another from attacks by sea, while the third side they could keep almost undefended.

Turks had slowly been gathering at the foot of Constantinople since the month of February because Mehmed wanted to sap the confidence of defenders through psychological pressure and to force them to surrender. For a full sixty days the soldiers had been arriving, cannons had been placed, tents built, galleys sailing in. Once mighty Byzantium had been crumbling and falling apart under Ottoman pressure for a hundred years already, like a full moon that is trimmed down into a thin sickle in phases. And then Mehmed, like Earth's shadow in some magical and impossible eclipse (because a lunar eclipse is only possible on nights of a full moon when high tides and bad forces rise up), swallowed almost the whole sickle, leaving only a tiny triangle at the very end like the tip of a spear. And now a shadow hung over the triangle, too. After a two-month-long parade and encampment Mehmed decided to shake the city walls. At dawn on April 7 the cannonade began. The cannons' shells split the *bluish half-darkness* like meteors. At daybreak on the horizon a pale lunar sickle and the morning star, or Venus, the mother of Aeneas, were watching. But Mehmed's strategy of exhaustion had another side as well, invisible like the dark side of the moon. In fact, after a wait interwoven with doubt and uncertainty that often transforms into a phantom of disunity and nervous intolerance, this series of cannon explosions sounded like a drum calling the besieged citizens to gather. And, during the previous years, the walls had been built and added on to like the crucial protection of a final shelter, like armor for the heart, a most secret chamber, an altar or sanctum sanctorum, some medieval version of a nuclear shelter. The most well known Byzantine men had thought of a way to protect one side of the city walls from even the mere possibility of attack. They did this by installing that chain at the entrance to the Golden Horn. So in a military sense the city de facto formed a corner, whose sides were faced one by the land, the other by the sea, while its imagined arch was nowhere. Put differently, Mehmed had to enter the gaping jaws of a crocodile in such a way as to break one of the jaws because he could not approach the mouth. But it seemed that the cannon shells were bouncing off the hard crocodile skin, both those from the true cannons as well as those from the small ship barrels. Mehmed, though, must have known that though his cannons were not for nothing they could not turn walls into ashes very fast. The salvos, therefore, continued, and for seven days a meteoritic rain was revealing and welcoming the waning moon and

Venus in two reincarnations: morning star and evening star. When the cannons became silent at night, the ears could not get used to the silence for a long while, and perhaps there was firing even in dreams. Still, it almost seemed that all of this was harder on the besieging troops than on the besieged. For that reason, on the seventh night after the evening prayer the sultan ordered the vizier to go on the attack the following day before the muezzin's call for morning prayer, while the defenders were not yet expecting even cannon salvos. And so it was. But sieges like these cannot be won by schoolboy tricks. For the first time the most serene ruler was looking at loss, retreat, and the crestfallen return of his men. The Byzantines had showered his foot soldiers and cavalry with tremendous fire, showing that they did not lack for ammunition and that they would try to force the sultan to realize that Constantinople is not worth a dead army and so to give up his siege and conquest. But for Mehmed there was no question of wavering. Because his namesake Mehmed the Prophet (let God's mercy be on him) had already called on the Byzantine emperor to accept Islam and it was high time for the muezzin's prayer to echo in this city. The attacks continued. Already that same day two new onslaughts ended up in the same way. On the following few days, the stamping of boots and horseshoes took over the fruitless role of cannonades. By now it was obvious that flesh is more fragile than walls. The shells were having no effect. People were getting killed. Every day the same attacks were beaten back from the city walls routinely and methodically, like the Bosporus waves breaking on the European and Asian shores. After twelve days of futile onslaughts the Ottoman army succeeded in getting a ladder on the city walls. But a rain of stones, a torrent of hot water and melted tar together with the familiar firing met those who started climbing. They had to retreat. That night Mehmed had to realize that his biggest (seeming) success had brought him his biggest (real) losses. Because missed opportunities, unlike dead bodies, are not counted. And after several more days of this even the dead would not be counted. Things could not continue this way. But it could not be different either. For several days from the Bosporus side Mehmed tried to get his soldiers to climb from the galleys up the city walls, but the defenders' fire did not even allow the ships to approach the fortified walls. So by the end of

April déjà vu onslaughts continued with almost expected failure. But the reduced confidence and militancy of the attackers did not shake the zeal and accuracy of the Byzantine shooters. Days differed from one another only in the meteorological scene, but neither fog nor rain helped the Turks. At the beginning of May, probably tormented, Mehmed again blanketed the city with an uninterrupted three-day cannonade. But it seems that the defenders needed the rest too. They decimated the next onslaught. In the following five days the number of victims increased, and the number that gives meaning to and is at the base of the frequency after which the verb "to decimate" is named, was reduced. From what began as an emotional and statistical problem the number of dead became a strategic and hygienic one. In fact, for Mehmed there was no military sentiment anymore, nor did he still insist that the dead be counted in order to compare daily losses. The sultan had to be afraid that if the attacks were to go on, even if he finally vanquished and put Constantinople *ad acta,* he could run out of *live bodies* for further planned conquests. And he was tormented by the only aspect of death somewhat separable from the metaphysical: the technical-hygienic problem of burial. There were so many dead that they could not keep up with burying them. If this pace continued there was the threat of the grotesque possibility that the siege would have to be stopped due to the stench of corpses and animal carcasses. Mehmed again decided to stop cavalry and infantry attacks for several days. He did not even order a new cannonade. He issued an order to fire a few shells occasionally so that the army would not forget that it was at war. Maybe he needed to think. Noise interferes with thinking. So in mid-May, after six weeks of hellish commotion in Constantinople and the camp of its conquerors, the impression of a truce began to spread. Those rare explosions that occasionally disturbed the now unnatural silence, in which horses' neighs and the noise of cauldrons became noise again, seemed like real thunder. With the influx of the dead having temporarily stopped, the wounded acquired the right to be noticed. It seems that only now they allowed themselves to wail and sob, when their fate no longer had the label of a second-class outcome compared to those who were lucky. Everything looked like those first April days when the whole Turkish force had just encamped at the foot of Constantinople but had not yet begun attacking. Only the landscape of emotions had changed sides. The defenders were now preoccupied with elated waiting, while the conquerors were ruled by nervousness and suspense. Just as sweet hope used to force Turkish eyes every so often to look for a white flag—a sign of surrender—on the city walls, so now were Byzantine eyes looking constantly for signs of a retreat. And the weather did not change: the sky and earth joined in the humid grayness of evil spring. The rare sun's golden rays that pierced the awning of clouds fell on fertile soil like God's mercy on the head of the righteous. On the beaten and trampled soil of the Ottoman encampment the only vegetation was the clumped and choppy turf of last year's yellowish grass, like an old man's beard almost fused together with mud and clay. A few scattered trees stood naked crying toward the sky with the scraggly branches, like prisoners with raised arms. Even the frightened birds bypassed the arena, all but the ravens. The winds deposited dust and restlessness. The smoke of camp kitchens burned the eyes and elicited coughing. The air stank with puss, dung, corpses, urine, sulfur, gunpowder, and sweat.

As always when he was nervous and thinking feverishly, Mehmed's forehead was sprinkled with sweat. In this tense interlude the days passed quickly. This unspoken cease-fire had already swallowed a whole week. May came to its last third. Hundreds of times every day Mehmed measured the royal tent with his steps. In the interludes he ate, prayed, and tried to sleep. Occasionally he would go out just to touch with his sight the mighty silhouette of the walls, to spit and curse. In a single moment his face would change expressions from anger to sadness, militancy, furious cruelty, dreary sympathy, and painful surprise as in a short pantomime of Achilles in the *Iliad.* But Achilles was powerless when faced with Troy. Mehmed spent a few more days in periodic mood swings. But then one morning while eating smoked meat for breakfast, he jumped up and with his mouth full called for the vizier to be brought before him. He ordered him to return to Turkey with a small detachment and to take from the people there several thousand sheep and to slaughter them, leaving the meat and skin to the owners. The vizier's glassy eyes revealed a horrified lack of comprehension. But the sultan's next words elicited an expression of perplexity on the face of his subordinate. As if in some apocryphal version of the myth of Prometheus, he was supposed to take the suet and to bring a sea of suet to the gates of Constantinople, not to the Turkish camp but to the other side of the Golden Horn, behind the Byzantine barriers and the first row of hills. On top of that, he had to task another detachment with finding planks, miles of planks. *So that I can pave the camp with them, if I want to*—so the sultan said. And the planks needed to be brought to the same place as the suet and all of it in three days. The sultan's eyes were shining.

After the vizier crossed to Asia with the two detachments, Mehmed ordered the galleys from the Bosporus to begin docking on the shores of the Turkish camp and the army to begin boarding. When the Byzantines saw the first overflowing galley (the surface of the deck was not even visible because of the number of the Turks) heading north, saw it disappear behind the blocked entrance to the Golden Horn and then, sailing the strait, get ever more distant from Constantinople, they started celebrating. The bells of the Church of Agia Sophia tolled without a break for three days, for the last time. Young men at the tops of the city's towers counted the departing galleys. Twenty of them sailed away on the first day. In the general Constantinople celebration, a clergyman named Lazarus, who dared to call for caution and a bit more patience, was mocked. The next day thirty new ships sailed away, even more laden it seemed (if that was possible) than those of the previous day. On the third day no one counted the departing ships anymore. All of them had sailed off by dusk. At the site of the former Ottoman encampment only the cannons remained, along with a small part of the Ottoman army for which there was no space on the galleys. The Byzantines were of two minds as to whether these would stay there as a kind of mock siege or whether some of the galleys would return for them the next day. But it seems they were not really interested in this at all. At twilight, the remaining Turks blazed away with the most furious cannonade on the city walls yet, and for the first time at night—out of frustration perhaps. For the revelers in the city it was almost a pleasant accompaniment to their pent-up joy. But pretty much at the time of the beginning of the Byzantine celebration (a bit after the first departing ship had disappeared over the horizon from the defenders) the Turks started to disembark. The galleys docked at the spot where the sultan expected the vizier's return. At early evening of the third day at almost the same time, the final ships and the vizier with the suet and the planks arrived. Then the sultan gave an order that echoed among the soldiers as simultaneously a vision of victory and a sign of royal madness. During the night the narrow spit of flat land under the hills had to be de facto paved with the planks, and then where the wooden trail crossed an imagined point parallel to the final edge of the city and barriers, a bend had to be made and the paving had to be continued all the way to the shore of the Golden Horn. After that the wooden trail was to be made slippery by spreading suet over it. Simply put, instead of digging a canal Mehmed had decided to build a bridge, a bridge over which his ships could sail. After twilight when the cannons on the other side began the nightly fusillade, the Ottoman army anthill began laying down the beams that settled into the soft soil like bricks into mortar. From the shore of the improvised Bosporus dock toward the shore of the bay that had temporarily been turned into something like a salty lake by the Byzantine chains, a strange road was created in a shape of reversed letter "L," around the hills and barriers. It was clear. The full moon shone like a silver sun. The warm night was finally indicating the arrival of true spring, that spring that is dearer and sweeter to the heart than any summer. When the road was finished, it was covered with suet like asphalt sprinkled with salt in winter. But now the ships were supposed to sail on land. The soldiers tied strong ropes to the galleys and pulled them one by one over the planks. The Roman Empire became what it was with the help of galley slaves from the East; now with the help of Eastern galley slaves (somewhat different) it would be finally and completely destroyed. Before sunrise all the galleys had been launched into the waters of the Golden Horn. The sun in all its glory started rising over Constantinople when the Turks began to climb the weakest, undefended walls. It was the morning of May 29, 1453. There was almost no resistance. Everything was over before evening. Constantine XI was killed like Romulus Augustus. Mehmed gained the title *Fatih*—the Conqueror. On the wings of this victory he conquered Moldavia, Serbia, the Morea, and Trabizon. And, precisely ten years after conquering Constantinople, on May 29, 1463, he arrived in the vicinity of a city that had been, like Constantinople, created for defense. At the narrowest part of a canyon made by a gold-bearing small river on a green highland there was an unconquerable, and, up to the last turn also invisible, fortress, in which Mehmed, perhaps in some kind of prophetic dream, could see one minaret, and on the greenish-blue background of the landscape six more. Unlike the Roman emperors the founders of Travnik did not dream up announcements suitable to cigarette ads, but they knew all three symbols. For that reason Mehmed was able to put Mohammed's flag on the fortress in only four days. Then, on the flat land behind the fortress, next to one of an infinite number of springs of the most beautiful water on earth, after having had a ritual wash, he prayed the noon prayer. Later, the Colorful Mosque was built at that spot, unique due to the fact that its minaret is oriented toward the East.

The person telling this story got the idea to do so in the following way. It happened one evening when he sat tired on a wooden bench next to the Colorful Mosque. *Those were hot summer days, but the nights were cool.* He lit a cigarette and watched the water flowing. The man was sweaty, and he rubbed the planks of the wooden bench with his palms. His hands glided smoothly over wood that was greasy like suet from sweat and salty like seawater or the froth from which Venus was born. It was pleasant and strange to touch the wood, the wood greasy and slippery, on which ships can sail. *They understood each other immediately. Then he decided to write its history.*

Translated from the Bosnian by Oleg Andrić and Andrew Wachtel

■ □ ■ □ ■

THE THRESHOLD OF MATURITY

Men must endure
Their going hence, even as their coming hither;
Ripeness is all.

William Shakespeare via Joseph Brodsky

Fruits are ripe when they are plump
Like a blue corpse
Like ink on graduation diplomas,
When their taste and color are completely foreseeable,
Like B movies.

Muhamed Dženetić

A measure of maturity: the ability to resist symbols. But, humanity is getting younger and younger.

Milan Kundera

PAVEL SAW MARTINA FOR THE FIRST TIME IN FRONT OF THE MOVIE theater Hvezda one May twilight in 1994. Pavel was a twenty-three-year-old student of film directing at the famous FAMU, a senior. Peter Weir's movie *Gallipoli* was being shown that evening. Pavel liked Peter Weir's movies. In one popular culture magazine he had recently published an essay about Weir's aesthetics under the title "Australian Gospel." Because, for Pavel, Peter Weir was truly the only *good news* from Australia. When on one occasion he did an improvised poll among his colleagues about what came to their minds when the words Australia and culture were mentioned, he got only two answers: INXS and Nick Cave. One of Pavel's student projects was a short film, *The Sixth Continent: Kangaroos and Convicts,* inspired exactly by this informal poll. The film consisted exclusively of answers given by numerous members of the so-called educated population to the question: *What do you know about Australia?* The quality and quantity of knowledge were catastrophic: the title summarizes them precisely. His film won first prize at the International Festival of Student Movies in Sidney. At the beginning of the movie there was an epigraph taken from an essay by Kundera: *Uniting the history of the planet, that humanistic dream which God gloatingly allowed to happen, is followed by a process of reduction.*

Pavel's student films were completely different from the ones made by his colleagues and contemporaries. While the films made by the majority of the students tended to be somewhat political or to deal with the fallout from the collapse of the iron curtain, Pavel's works carried a certain lyrical sensibility, completely unpolluted by any trace of politics. What is more, the disappearance of any kind of censorship was primarily used by young directors to present different themes touching on sexuality, and their films most often uncovered a cruel world of sensuality and the flesh, a world that melted into a kind of wanton debauchery. Pavel's, on the contrary, had an almost Victorian *air* about them, a dualistic asceticism, and a troubadour-like vision of male-female relationships. On the formal plane his films had a *sensibility of challenging literariness,* as one of his professors said on some occasion. Pavel, though, was beloved at the academy as a great talent, and particularly much was expected from the film he was making as his graduation project. It was an adaptation of Kundera's novella *The Hitchhiking Game,* a novella that incorporated both a thematic closeness to Pavel's already recognizable *signature* and a narrative simplicity necessary for the realization of the film on the financial side.

It is easy to notice Pavel's affinity with the work of Milan Kundera, a closeness that was, perhaps, not as natural as it might seem at first sight. Because, after the transition, the émigré dissidents were not all that well accepted. But Pavel's affinity with Kundera's work (or with parts of his work, the parts where *Laughable Loves,* or *The Hitchhiking Game,* belong) had begun in the early days of his youth, because the spring fervor of his parents did not completely turn into ketman;[1] their external loyalty did not become a Kafkaesque desire for their own guilt. The kind who had, on the contrary, removed dissident books from the family libraries did not get them back nor acquire their newer works. The only even somewhat political film Pavel made was called *My Generation: Murti-Bing.* It consisted of summaries and clips from the films of his colleagues, followed by the text of the first chapter of *The Captive Mind* by Czesław Miłosz, a book dealing with self-censorship at the time of communism. The paradoxical moral of the story was that *a captive mind is a captive mind, regardless of what captivates it.* With this movie Pavel's unpopularity among his colleagues increased even more, although it might have seemed that it had already reached its zenith. Among the other students Pavel was always known as an odd person, because he did not live the life of a typical artist, because he was not a slave to that old-fashioned bohemian style usually considered the necessary backdrop for creativity.

It was in front of the theater Hvezda then, that Pavel noticed Martina. But he still did not know her name. She was just a good-looking green-eyed girl in light white dress accompanied by a younger girlfriend, almost a little girl. Pavel was alone. He always went to the movies alone, ever since his high school days. At that time, when the darkness of a movie theater betokened idleness, and not, as was the case now, an evocation of the darkness of a church at twilight, he had gone with Mihaela. Mihaela was Pavel's girlfriend for more than three years, the only girl he dated *seriously.* But they did not go to watch movies, they went to kiss. Kisses in a movie theater are the most shameless kisses; in the acoustic hall the smack of lips echoes like the calling of a nymph in love. The darkness of a movie theater is not the darkness of a street, a movie theater is *dark with something more than night.* But his relationship with Mihaela, a relationship overburdened by puberty's phantom of eternity, broke up in a fairly operatic way. One afternoon he found her, actually, in the arms of Aleš, her contemporary and a school friend. She had always pointed to their friendship as her own affirmative example during those nighttime half-drunk conversations when *eternal* topics such as whether a man and a woman could be *just* friends are rehashed. Even as a child Pavel had memorized Chekhov's (apropos, Pavel's short potpourri on themes taken from three of Chekhov's short stories was called *If Polanski Is Polish Then Chekhov Is Czech*) witticism about the *phases on the road of life* in relationships between a woman and a man, that famous line that says that to a man a woman could first be an acquaintance, then a lover, and only then, at the end, after those two phases, as a culmination—a friend. But what made this event vaudevillian was the fact that on the same day he found Mihaela, as it were, in flagrante with Aleš, he came in contact with that witticism three times: first, a professor talking about Chekhov mentioned a gun, the first and third act, and the observation about friendship between a man and a woman, then he, reading the newspaper, found this phrase in some political commentary as the icing on the cake to some paradoxical commentary of a columnist, and then, finally, in some trivial TV movie he watched while eating lunch, one of the characters used this quote from Chekhov, attributing it to Oscar Wilde. This multiplication of bizarre coincidences disturbed Pavel in some strange way; he was perhaps overcome by that *ineradicable dread common to all human beings (and possibly even to the more intelligent animals), which suddenly seizes them, when as a result of some chance events they begin to doubt the* principium individuationis, *in that the principle of sufficient reason seems to undergo an exception. For example, when it appears that some event has occurred without a cause, or a deceased person seems to be alive again, or when in some other way the past or future is present, or the distant is near.* He consoled himself perhaps with Hamlet's sophism about the fall of a sparrow, and he tried to play down the significance of the repetition, but he remained agitated, and his agitation said: *her relationship with Aleš is at a more advanced level than her relationship with me.* When he found them in that pose of intimacy, the only pose that made him special in her life, he felt almost relieved, although the lack of confirmation of his turbulent doubt would completely remove any value from that repetition and turn it into a simple coincidence. Every love has its passwords. The love of Pavel and Mihaela had two. Pavel never wore gloves and in the winter Mihaela would give him her left glove, keeping the right one for herself. Since they would be holding hands (her left in his right hand), they did not notice the absence of one glove because they would heat each other's naked palms. On winter nights this would prompt Pavel to make lucid, albeit somewhat ironic declamations about the harmony of the universe, declamations that recalled the joke of Groucho Marx (that American

Marx, the symbol of the mocking lightness of the New World versus the pathetically serious European heaviness embodied by *Herr* Karl), who when asked *Why do people have five fingers?* answers *If they had six, the glove makers would go out of business!* Both Pavel and Mihaela loved the band the Smiths and considered "Hand in Glove" to be *their song.* Also they exchanged copies of their birth certificates instead of photographs and carried them in their wallets in place of photographs. Three months after that fatal day (a period during which, after Aleš, Mihaela replaced at least as many *cavaliers* as there are fingers on a glove) Pavel wrote a paragraph from Kierkegaard on the back of her birth certificate, which he still carried like a talisman: *I do not like girls. Their beauty passes like a dream and like a day that is over. Their faithfulness—yes, their faithfulness! They are either unfaithful; that does not interest me anymore, or they are faithful. If I were to find such a faithful soul, I would value it as a rarity, but with the passing of time I would not like it anymore; because she would either remain faithful forever and I would become a victim of my own desire for experiments since I would have to stay with her to the end, or the moment would come when she would stop being faithful, and then the old story would repeat itself.*

For almost four years Pavel had remained faithful to this quote. Girls did not disappear from his life completely, but he *did not like them.* But now he observed the young green-eyed girl as if he liked her. Still, when the audience began to enter the theater, Pavel forgot the girl like a believer who forgets the things of this world at the church door. *Pray not to fall into temptation because the spirit is willing but the flesh is weak*—Christ said in Gethsemane. And just as the Lord in church might test a zealous believer by seating an attractive beauty in the pew next to him, so did destiny in the form of the ticket salesman seat Pavel and Martina on two neighboring chairs. At the moment that the lights were dimming, he felt the quick light touch of a warm rounded knee. But the movie began, the mass began, and Pavel was far away again: in Australia, in Egypt, and finally in Gallipoli. In the last scene, when the flower of Australian youth went to their death, an adagio began, Albinoni's Adagio, that divine ode to metaphysical death, to the youthful feeling of death distant from flesh and blood and all that is bodily, to that death that is a completely spiritual, intellectual perception of Novalis's bluish nonexistence, composed of *such stuff as dreams are made of* like life or the Maltese falcon. And then Pavel had to experience that feeling that visited him occasionally on some spring days, a feeling that Camus compares *to certain evenings when the heart is resting,* and Miłosz to *the sun's light and the earth's smell,* a feeling that in his diary on May 19, 1838, Kierkegaard called an *indescribable joy.* But the lights came up again and Pavel became aware of the presence of the green-eyed girl. In a trance he addressed her, they introduced themselves (she was called, of course, Martina, and the little girl was her sister Milena), and Pavel went by inertia outside with them talking and talking as if drugged.

Do you know, do you know (unconsciously he was already addressing only Martina) *how many soldiers the army of the British Empire lost at Gallipoli? Thirty-four thousand! And only seven thousand graves are known! What happened to the twenty-seven thousand men who were left without graves, even without cenotaphs? And there is the testimony of three New Zealanders who described the charge of an Australian battalion on which a large black cloud descended. When the cloud lifted there was nobody there. Nobody! Official reports mention the fog that helped the Turks destroy the unit, but even from a decimated unit the corpses remain at least. Here nobody remained. Nobody! The film talks about that unit. For sure! Because Weir is obsessed with disappearances. Did you watch his* Picnic at Hanging Rock*? You did! Then you surely remember that it is a true story about the disappearance of a few girls from a boarding school, a disappearance that remained a mystery forever. Weir knows that disappearance, the disappearances of people are a fundamental phenomenon of our age. But he talks about the lyrical moment of disappearance, about metaphysical disappearances, hints at those official, institutional disappearances in concentration camps. He talks from the innocent and naive perspective of the Bermuda triangle, but it is up to us to anticipate Auschwitz. Because in our time even death is not death anymore. Death is disappearance.*

He gasped. Martina looked at him worshipfully. She began to talk about *Dead Poets Society,* about *Witness,* "Captain, My Captain," and "Don't Know Much about History." They interrupted each other, they laughed. She said she also watched *The Year of Living Dangerously* and *The Plumber. What do you know about Australia?*—he asked her. *James Cook, Abel Tasman, Van Diemen . . .*—she started at random. *That's enough!*—Pavel said laughingly. She had read Kundera, she had the first edition of *The Joke*. In forty minutes he walked them to their door. *How old are you?*—he managed to ask her at parting. *Seventeen.*

Somewhat later that same night Pavel awoke, rid himself of his almost forgotten and then shortly resurrected love trance. Perhaps he considered everything to be just a product of a strange set of circumstances. As if during the several hours since parting from Martina several years had in fact passed, as if during that time he had aged and could almost say, à la Kundera: *I was overwhelmed by a tide of anger at myself, anger at my own age then, that stupid lyrical age.* Just as, in the moments immediately after parting he could have been angry with himself because he did not ask her to see him again, so now from the same reason he could have been happy.

He saw her again one late July morning about forty days later. She was alone. Under her arm she carried a phonograph record. He approached her and invited her for coffee. They sat down in a small cafeteria nearby, a place Pavel frequented every day. After he cordially greeted the waiter, Martina asked him to request that they play the record she was carrying. The café was anachronous enough and still had a record player. It was *The Doors* record, that posthumous record of Jim Morrison from which since the moment it appeared he sang and recited *from the other side,* the album *An American Prayer.* Pavel loved Morrison because Morrison too studied at a film school and also because of the fact that Morrison's first book of poems in prose *Lords* was almost completely devoted to thoughts about movies. He answered the poll *Why I make movies?* by some cinematic magazine concerned with reduced public interest in art films with a quote from this book, quoted in the original: *It is wrong to assume that art needs the spectator in order to be. The film runs on without any eyes. The spectator cannot exist without it. It ensures his existence.* But the waiter put on the record and the deep voice was heard reciting the emphatic point of the poem after which the album was named, the point named *The Severed Garden,* accompanied by the only music worthy of verses *about death that makes angels of us all and gives us wings where we had shoulders smooth as raven's claws:* Albinoni's Adagio. Pavel was trembling as if in a fever. They drank coffee and smoked in shared silence, that most radical form of intimacy. At parting they quarreled about the bill. When Martina took out her wallet her own photograph fell out. Pavel picked it up and offered a compromise. She could pay but only if she gave him the photograph. She agreed. Again he saw her to her door. When they parted she mentioned that in two days she was traveling to Spain with her parents, her brother, and her sister (in addition to her younger sister Milena, whom he had already met, she also had an elder brother, František), and she hoped that on her return they would see each other again.

When he arrived home he looked at Martina's photograph for a long time. She looked transparent, immaterial like some purely spiritual form of existence from sci-fi literature, like an astral projection or a hologram. It must have been then that he remembered that song sung by the singer with the melancholy voice, Tanita (whose name, with its mixture of alliteration and irregular assonant rhyme, recalls that of Kundera's favorite female name: Tamina), the song in whose refrain she compares her own eyes to holograms. He must have remembered that song because on the back of Martina's photograph—like Baudelaire who on the back of the photograph of his *black Venus* wrote words from the First Epistle of Saint Peter *Quaerens quem devore* (Searching for whom to devour) taken from that saint's saintly appeal for caution that says: *Be sober and watch: because your enemy the devil, like a roaring lion, goes about searching for whom to devour*—he wrote one of her verses: *up in arms and chaste and whole.*

He met her for the third time in mid-August. Her skin was tanned and her hair bleached. It was early morning. Pavel liked to walk the empty streets in the early mornings, and so, it turned out, did Martina. She had returned from Spain the day before, and she went out to take a walk, full of the internal happiness of the return, the most beautiful part of any trip. They sat again in some just opened café where they were the first and, for now, the only customers. On a shelf above the bar the television set was turned on. They did not pay any attention to the programming until the sobs of Albinoni's Adagio began to pour forth from the screen. On some Bosnian ruin a large cellist in a black suit was playing the Adagio. They looked at it disbelievingly. Perhaps in order to just say something, Pavel mentioned a Bosnian poet whom he liked: Muhamed Dženetić. Martina nodded: she had read him. They talked about Dženetić's great love for his wife, a love that was replaced by his passion for Venice after her death. Martina wanted to return home before her folks woke up. He saw her to the already known door, kissing her without a word at parting. He deliberately said nothing. *Words are something else; words, words, words.* Everything that is immortal was born in silence. And it is not an accident that in fairy tales a vow of silence is a commonplace. *Silence is the Great Brahman.* Silence is the most beautiful *ex voto. A man is more of a man because of the things he keeps silent than the things he says. The rest is silence.*

(Muhamed Dženetić wrote:

Every bridge has its own angel
And no words are needed for it
Because it is for an angel to carry a message
And prevent the lack of silence

If love is something it is a bridge
There is no love as soon as you look for words
Because a bridge without an angel is not a footbridge
Nor is love a kiss without a angel

When he came home he took Martina's photograph from his wallet (it was placed over the copy of Mihaela's birth certificate). He looked at it for a long time thinking perhaps about that Chekhovian phrase and about the fact that it is *always easy to be logical, but it is almost impossible to be completely logical.* Because that aphorism does not mention that extremely radical and most rare possibility, the possibility that the woman can become the man's sister. Perhaps for that reason under the verse *up in arms and chaste and whole* he wrote the title of a song of the band the Cult, a song he did not like, but a song whose title became the password to his heart with the premonition of its sense and alliteration: "Sweet Soul Sister." Then he returned the photograph to his wallet.

At the beginning of September, when Pavel saw an announcement for the film *Night Train to Venice* in the movie theater Blanik, he decided to see it. The film was hardly attractive to him (it was just one of the seasonal half-hits that would be consigned to *laughter and forgetting*), but he wanted to see it, perhaps because of the city in the title. In front of the movie theater that evening he kept looking around and he stood on the balls of his feet as if waiting for someone, though he only bought one ticket. He entered the theater as if bewildered. An instant before the lights were turned off he heard some kind of commotion and pushing a few rows behind him. Someone was late for the movie; actually that someone had arrived exactly on time, but there are places where not to be a little bit early is the same as being late; you cannot arrive for church as if for gunfight, *at high noon.* He turned around. The late arrivals were Martina, her sister Milena, and some young man, perhaps their brother. This is when he saw her for the fourth time. The lights were turned off. The movie was unimaginative, bad, and boring. Pavel almost did not watch it. He turned around frequently in order to sight Martina, in order for Martina to sight him. But the movie takes place in a night train, the silver screen, that only sun in a movie theater, was dark, and its darkness made the theater's darkness look like that of a grave, like a photographic darkroom. But a moment before the end of the movie, when the morning shone on the silver screen and the theater darkness became less thick, the Adagio resounded as the musical background for a scene that must have reminded Pavel of his classmates' movies. But as a background to the stereo acoustics of the powerful hidden speakers Pavel could also hear the well-known smacking of lips similar to the voice of a nymph in love, he could hear it live, *live.* Perhaps even before he turned around he could have known that Martina was playing Mihaela, and that her purported brother was playing his youthful incarnation. For the first time in his life he left the theater before the end of a film, he left church before the end of the sermon. Together with the tramp of his steps the sounds of the Adagio died down as well.

When he arrived home (it was past midnight already) he pulled from a drawer the synopsis for a film he intended to make, a film he had always insisted would be his first *mature* work. It was supposed to be a film devoted to his own city, which he intended to be the first person to see from a completely new perspective, at least it seemed this way to him. He lit a cigarette and began reading aloud, slowly, to himself.

Prague—city of mysteries, city of dreams that get lost in other dreams, city in which everything is possible like in the dusky foggy

London of Robert Browning. It is the city in which a warning to the human race will have echoed three times, a warning that unites the crucial events in the life of Saint Peter, heavenly key holder and symbol both of human weakness and strength. Because the warning will have echoed three times, just as Peter renounced Christ three times before the cock started crowing, and the warning is identical to the question that same Peter asked the resurrected Christ: Quo vadis? *Three times in Prague there would appear the symbol of humanity's future, the symbol of modern man. Three times it will have appeared in the human spirit before it crosses over into reality. In the spirit of Gustav Meyrink it will have appeared like Golem, in the spirit of Franz Kafka like Odradek, and, finally, in the spirit of Karl Čapek (and a bit later in reality too) like a robot. The same premonition of dehumanization appeared in Italy under the mask of a fairy tale about Pinocchio, in Geneva as a novel about Frankenstein, and in the Caribbean in the form of legend about zombies; but Prague is the city where this premonition found its home.*

Pavel stopped reading and went to the window. It began to drizzle. Pavel caressed the windowsill splashed with soggy pigeon droppings. He lit another cigarette. And while he smoked, looking at the roofs of his city, Pavel continued to stroke the windowsill (in the intervals between bringing the cigarette to the lips) with the hand in which he held the cigarette. In the other hand he held the text of his synopsis. He skipped two or three pages and began to read another paragraph.

If death is the last act of maturing then in Prague a windowsill is the threshold of maturity. Because perhaps exclusively thanks to Prague there exists that bizarre word that means to throw someone out a window, a word to which Arthur Clarke devoted one of his stories: defenestration. But ever since the first defenestration, the citizens of Prague generally threw themselves out of windows.

Pavel leaned out the window. The street was empty. The rain had stopped, but it was still late (or early). Everything was quiet. Pavel drummed on the windowsill with his fingers as if he was recovering from the last four months of his life, his four meetings with Martina like four movements of his summer symphony, pathetic but not unfinished, a symphony with the leitmotif of the Adagio. Dawn was already breaking when Pavel closed the window and went to sleep.

When the first ray of sun fell on his face he was lying with closed eyes and it seemed as if he was smiling. Perhaps it seemed to him or he dreamed that someone was passing by on the street beneath the window. Someone walking slowly whistling the Adagio.

Translated from the Bosnian by Oleg Andrić and Andrew Wachtel

■ □ ■ □ ■

A RED FLOWER FOR TOMISLAV PODGORAĆ

EVERY YEAR ON THE NIGHT OF JANUARY 19 A MYSTERIOUS MALE FIGURE visits the cemetery near the former Westminster Hall Church in Baltimore. The man is dressed in a black raincoat, he has a dark hat pulled down over his forehead, and around his neck is a white scarf. Every January 19 between midnight and dawn the mysterious man approaches the grave of Edgar Allan Poe and places three red roses and a half-empty bottle of Martel cognac on it. I do not know whether anyone ever visits the grave of Tomislav Podgorać in Paris, but I like to imagine that it is occasionally visited by a young man wearing dark glasses, black pants and a black shirt, and a black corduroy jacket, with long black somewhat wavy hair. His jacket pockets are very deep, and in the right one, together with a pack of cigarettes and a Zippo lighter, a book could also fit comfortably. And in fact a thick book does protrude from the young man's right-hand pocket: either the Bible or Marx's *Capital*. In his hand is a red flower: either a rose like the ones on Poe's grave, a rose with a thorny stem like Jesus's crown, or a carnation with which workers decorate themselves for May 1 celebrations, a symbol of loving longing in lyrical Bosnian love songs.

Tomislav Podgorać was born in September of 1906, in a village near Našice. His father was a village teacher, a wizard of literacy in that little corner of Pannonia. When Tomislav was himself ready to start attending school, to add an official part to the intimate relationship with his own father, World War I began. That summer and fall of Anno Domini 1914 Tomislav watched his father's former students as, after sad drunken village parties, they were leaving families, young wives or fiancées, and going to the army. For the most part, they were not coming back. And while every morning, with a mixture of hope and fear, the parents of missing young men waited for the mailman, hoping for an envelope with a symbol of the Red Cross and a letter from their son from some prison camp where, alive and well, he was waiting for the end of the war, and fearing a telegram with condolences from the emperor, their intended and unintended daughters-in-law, the wives and fiancées of their sons, were flirting with all kinds of county notaries and other civil servants of the king and emperor, with millers and well-to-do sons, with old men and young boys, with any males outside the royal uniformed class. In those years in the rich flatlands flour was measured in tablespoons, while sinful moans emanated from the haylofts. One Sunday the village priest cried out for the mangers to be left to the birthing labors of virgins and not to lewd desecration. Tomislav was spelling the first letters from the leather-bound Bible while, even in this small and obscure village, one could sense the unpleasant smell of the tanning skin of the world, the physiological anticipation of the psychoanalytic theory of eros and thanatos, the strange mixture of the reek of soldiers' purulent skin and the sweaty stink of the wanton reddish skin of unconfirmed and unsure yet expectant widows, though legally still married women, those whom the ancient Hebrew law calls *agunot,* the wives of missing, the wives of those whose corpses and graves are unknown, the wives of those and other unfortunates for whom the ancient Greeks built cenotaphs.

At the time that the end of the war could already be foreseen, Tomislav Podgorać went to Osijek to attend the classical gymnasium. Before his eyes, the furrows of Central European facades replaced the furrows of arable land in his native village. In the school building a portrait of the young regent with glasses and a thin mustache soon replaced the photograph of the old king and emperor with medals and sideburns. The beggars on the streets were not replaced. Tomislav regularly attended school and church, trying to synchronize his thirst for knowledge and for justice. And although the church vision of God's justice still ruled his being, something intruded on the uniform passivity and conformity of the opportunistic justice-loving imposed and preached by the priests, something that could easily be equated with a sense of justice in general. That something was in fact an earthquake, a distant echo of the ten-day October earthquake that shook the world. In fact, the communists won the first postwar elections in Osijek.

The early twenties of the twentieth century were a decisive period both for Tomislav Podgorać and the Communist Party of Yugoslavia, for a man and an institution whose bizarre relationship would last until his and its more or less simultaneous death. Tomislav Podgorać spent his last high school years reading somewhat disparate books: the Bible and the works of the atheistic philosophers from the nineteenth century, philosophers who, despite disavowing God, pleaded for peace, justice, and goodwill among humankind. At that time, the zealous Communist Party activists who were trying to turn the ideas of the dead contemplatives in Tomislav's private library into reality were being persecuted. But Tomislav, who was bothered by both the passivity of the church and the atheism of the revolutionaries, still considered that barriers could be both surmountable and insurmountable. He, though, like some theologians, considered lack of faith in God the only unforgivable sin and the only insurmountable barrier. For that reason, on Diderot's imaginary fork in the road between becoming a communist priest and a believing revolutionary he chose the former. Because a believing revolutionary has been a *contradictio in adjecto* since Prometheus. Upon graduating high school Tomislav Podgorać decided, after hard-won family approval, to join the apostolic community Society of Jesus.

The eighteen-year-old Tomislav Podgorać began studying scholastic philosophy in Zagreb. Erigenus, Berengar, Abelard, Bonaventure, Albert the Great, Lulius, Bacon, Thomas Aquinas are the names that frocked professors repeat like mantras and count like rosary beads during lectures, and their robes suggest the mass as the archetype of every instruction. But the holy Latin of the old scholastics from the dawn of European Christianity did not completely cover Tomislav's spiritual life like the morning sun on the horizon. A young man who, based on his description, could have been Tomislav Podgorać was regularly seen at Krleža's lectures and the premieres of his works. According to some testimonies, Tomislav Podgorać was that mysterious young man seen in some Zagreb bars in choleric quarrels with prominent communist illegals, for example with Antun Mavrak. A strange collection of books found in a Zagreb family library could be proof of the interests of young Podgorać in the modern literature of that time. Among a hundred or so titles there are various leather-bound critical editions of the works of scholastic philosophers in gothic type, as well as the first thin and cheap postwar editions of young poets. On the first page of each book there is an improvised ex libris in black ink: the stylized initials *T.P.* and below them *A.M.D.G.* Certain lines or verses in almost all the books were underlined in black ink, too. These nota bene of warnings, reminders of enchantment, and proofs of *close reading* were most prominent in two books: Saint Augustine's *Confessions* (Leipzig 1870) and Ivo Andrić's *Ex Ponto* (Zagreb 1918).

But numerous outside interests did not prevent Tomislav Podgorać from graduating first in his class. The topic of his graduation thesis *The Scholastic Philosophers' Disinterest in Social Questions as the Main Cause for Dualistic Heresies and the Reformation* could almost stand as a symbolic leitmotif of his life, just as it might have for Kierkegaard, who in *Either-Or,* as proof of his thesis *that a man, through all stages of his entire life, always deals in principle with the same things,* quotes one of his schoolboy works *about proofs of the existence of God, about the immortality of the soul, about the concept of faith, and about the meaning of miracles,* which he wrote as a fifteen-year-old. Having completed his studies the twenty-two-year-old graduate was supposed to undertake a pedagogic internship somewhere. Tomislav Podgorać was sent to Travnik as a *master teacher* for high school students.

Like Fr. Nikola Granić, who was nicknamed Mumin, Tomislav Podgorać was *an expert in language and a good role model for the young.* That was not the end of the similarity between the young Jesuit professor and Guča Gora's onetime Franciscan. Tomislav, like Nikola, was *handsome and stalwart,* and it is easy to imagine that some tradesman, some new *Rustan-aga, a market assayer,* when he saw him in Travnik's downtown, would say about him, as about Mumin: *What a burly friar, I do not praise his faith! Pity he is baptized! You could make two good imams out of him.* Tomislav Podgorać spent three years working in the Travnik High School and, just before his death in Paris, frequently pointed out precisely these three years as the most beautiful period of his stormy and long life. Perhaps it was only during these three years that his similarity to Fr. Nikola Granić had a connection with the *Turkish order,* that quiet praise of contemplativeness and observation, resigned acceptance of the imperfection of the world, and enjoyment of a small piece of the world, of one's own garden as opposed to the barren hubbub and tumult, the abyss of all kinds of great activities, failed attempts to improve humanity, and pretentious programs for *changing the world.*

Tomislav Podgorać liked to walk around Travnik. He was seen daily both in Šumeće and on Kalibunar. Just as in Denmark today mothers say to naughty children *Don't be a Soren!* so, too, some old woman in Travnik will say about a young man inclined to drifting and aimless walks that *he is exactly like the young priest.* Almost always he was alone and in thought, but occasionally a kind of shallow sociability bubbled forth from him, and it was impossible to know when he would stop and chat with someone. He was not choosy about his interlocutors, and was equally kind to beggars as he was to his own colleagues. Perhaps on some of his walks he stopped to chat with Muharem Bazdulj, my grandfather and namesake, who also walked around Travnik beaming, as if suspecting that in this town he would live and die, and that his son and daughter would be born here. In spite of his loneliness and unsociability Tomislav Podgorać had a specific talent for following the flow of the town's events and a kind of ingenuity for remembering physiognomies. He would always remember a man he had once seen, and more than once he recognized a blood relationship between people based on the similarity of their faces.

Podgorać's students all remembered him well. One of them described him as *an inspirational and talented speaker with a piercing look, who gave his lectures in a modulated bass baritone.* Once during a lecture some kind of digression led him to the territory of poetry. Talking about a sonnet and the height of sonnet mastery, reached only by Petrarch and Shakespeare, he mentioned that among the best sonnets he had read in *our* language were some from a small cycle, *Flowering Primroses,* that had been published last year in the almanac of the Travnik High School, *Croatian Nymph,* by a student, a Skender Kulenović. One day Tomislav Podgorać stopped the recent graduate Skender Kulenović on a bridge below the school to praise him and to advise him not to give up on poetry. Twelve years later in Zagreb it seemed to Skender that he saw *that priest of his* in a bar, but he thought he was wrong and that the man just looked like him, because, as he said later, *What kind of a priest would be in a proletarian bar?*

In Travnik Tomislav Podgorać began smoking. Until the end of his life he pointed to cigarettes as his only sensual satisfaction (always adding that smoking *is not just a physical pleasure*), and he surely considered this to be one additional gift given to him by Travnik. The butts of his numerous cigarettes melded with the soil beneath two clock towers and numerous minarets, under the fortress in the *old town,* on Bašbunar and on Bojna, on the trails by Lašva, on Gospa's spring, and in the grove behind the school. His letter from September of 1929, a letter sent to an unknown recipient in Zagreb, the only letter that is known for certain to have been written by Podgorać himself, firsthand and in the first person, gives a picture of this period of his life.

It is gorgeous here. I walk, read, drink coffee, and smoke. You know that I started smoking here. For me it is a kind of link with the world, with the earth—a link worth envying. Some local impressions are impossible to digest without a cigarette. When a man sits in Rudolf's café near Šumeće it is unhealthy not to light a cigarette. Especially since, given that he is seated in a café, from the very name of the institution it can be concluded that he is drinking coffee. Travnik people say: coffee without a cigarette is like a mosque without a minaret. *Apropos there are many minarets here. When you enter the town from the east you can see six or seven of them at a time. At the eastern entrance of town there is also a beautiful madrasah*[1] *building that, together with the building of the high school, is one of the most beautiful structures in town. The town is a fantastic and unheard of blend of Middle Eastern and Central European settlements. The main street could be moved to Zagreb without any changes, while some districts represent the original landscape of* A Thousand and One Nights. *I like the work. It is pleasant to teach these immature young men, almost children. The school library is surprisingly rich. Besides that, you know that I subscribe to the programs of numerous publishers and new books arrive for me almost daily. I read a lot, and I started learning English. In one of these modern series, I read a seemingly paradoxical thesis (I met with the precisely diametrically opposite one many times) that true poetry can always be translated into a different language without any loss of meaning, rhythm, and rhyme. I managed to translate that epigrammatic slogan of the Travnik folk into my English:* coffee without cigarette like mosque without minaret. *I cannot describe to you how much satisfaction this rendering has given to me. Travnik is a small town, but still it represents a kind of* navel of the world. *In these twenty-three years of mine, even before I came to Travnik, some of the most interesting people I knew were Travnik folks, just as a Travnik man is my favorite modern writer. An acquaintance of mine likes to say that Travnik is Bosnia's true major city, because only here was the seat of the Bosnian province and the vizier's court. It was from here also that the Dragon of Bosnia ruled (this name reminds me of the names of Indian tribal chiefs) during the few years of Bosnian independence. Foreign consuls were stationed here as in any other major city. According to the words of this acquaintance of mine this is one of the rare Yugoslav and European major cities. It is important to say precisely* major city, *because, as this man likes to say,* a major city and a capital city are two different things. *This is his* ceterum censeo. *Travnik folks' love for their native city is fascinating, too. This same acquaintance told me a story about some man born in the eighteenth century who lived through all possible troubles in Travnik and suffered unbelievably, but still he lived through it all and—as it is said here—endured it. He was known far and wide as a good rider, although he never left Travnik. But on one occasion he went somewhere on a trip and, just as he left Travnik behind, he fell off his horse (he, to fall off a horse!) and died right away. But what is most beautiful in this story is the fact that everybody knows that the man was named Ante, but his last name has been forgotten, although it is known for sure that it started with the letter S. So he was Ante S., that is Ante S, that is Antheus, the ancient titan, son of Earth, whose mother gave him immortality and strength as long as he stood on solid ground. Heracles could defeat him only by lifting him into the air. Ante S. from Travnik was a modern Antheus, whose native town was a mother, and who was immortal in its embrace, while he was completely weak and powerless anywhere else. Because here in the mosque walls the sparrows are nesting (I personally saw that a few days ago) just as the pigeons are settling in on the windows of the school church. This school was attended by a certain Petar Barbarić, who died in the Lord while still a student. Everyone here considers him a saint: Catholics, Orthodox, Muslims, and Jews in trouble equally visit his grave. On top of the hill Bojna, Jewish, Catholic, and Muslim cemeteries are next to each other. Only a fence separates them. I do not believe that anything similar exists even in Jerusalem. The Orthodox church and cemetery are somewhat lower down, in fact right next to the school. And in the town surrounding it, it is easy to find medieval Bosnian gravestones, the gravestones of the Bosnian heretics close to the Albigensians. Sometimes I go to the Franciscan monastery in Guča Gora (it is a village close to the town) and I have a talk with some of the little brothers. The monastery also has an interesting library, but just the sight of the building made of yellow stones set in a landscape of gentle greenery to the accompaniment of a sweet lazy cigarette is itself worth the long walk. Can you now at least partially understand how wonderful things are and how thankful I am to God for the goodness I feel, that goodness that unrefined people perhaps simply call youth?*

Three years later Tomislav Podgorać is in Zagreb again. He moves into the main Zagreb home of the Society of Jesus, into the residence on Palmotićeva Street. He works there as the assistant editor of the Jesuit magazine *Life*. His articles, published under the pseudonym Stephanus M., stand out from other texts published in the magazine in terms of both style and topic. The long, rhythmic, piercing, and aggressive sentences of Podgorać could almost be called Krležian. Even the topics were not too distant from Krleža's if we overlook the fact that these conflicts, unlike Krleža's, were written by the pen of a man who, like Descartes in the *Discourse on Method*, accepted as axiomatic only God's existence. In an article from January of 1932 published under the title *Lenin and Ivan Karamazov*, Stephanus M. advocates the thesis that the only sin of the Russian Bolshevik Revolution is its aggressive atheism. At the end of Podgorać's almost programmatic text it literally says: *Christianity and true communism are not only related and linked, but the two terms are also synonymous. The first Christians were true communists. And, just as, according to Plato, the first man was a hermaphrodite who was later halved into a man and a woman, so was the concept of true Christianity or communism split into the church and Bolshevism. The proletariat is the salt of the earth today, but Christianity lost the proletarians and they lost God. Only the devil won . . .*

After this text there were no more articles signed by Stephanus M. in *Life*. It could have been that the editorial board judged that young Tomislav had gone too far, but it is a fact also that for unknown reasons he was able even then to get away with going too far. It could be, then, that the reason was more prosaic than censorship. Perhaps in this text Podgorać said everything he wanted to say at that time, and perhaps his further writing was simply interrupted by preparations for a journey. Because in the spring of 1932 Tomislav Podgorać left Zagreb and went to Flanders, to Louvain, which at the time had the reputation as one of the best Catholic universities. Perhaps he wanted to try to calm in the lee of a university the justice-loving trance of his that could force him into unwanted thoughtlessness.

Tomislav Podgorać spent four years in Louvain. In the spring of 1936 he defended the first of the three doctorates he would get during his life. Less than a year earlier, in the summer of 1935, he was solemnly ordained into the priesthood, and he celebrated his first mass in the Church of the Holy Trinity in Cepin. After his doctoral program, he spent a year in the Flemish city of Tranchiennes doing in-depth final Jesuit preparation, and he was also the favorite leader of spiritual exercises among French and Belgian Catholic intellectuals. Podgorać's only preserved photograph is from that period, too. There are fifteen Jesuits in the photograph: six are seated, and nine are standing. They look like some kind of soccer team in frocks. Tomislav Podgorać is the *first from the left in the lower row.* He has crossed his arms in his lap and has straightened his right leg as if getting ready to stand up. In the background is a building with a brick facade and one large window over which a screen to keep out mosquitoes has been spread. On Tomislav's face is a kind of manly Giaconda-like smile, or more likely a grimace of quiet sadness rather than joy, an emblem of the *joy of grief.* This photograph recalls the description of Father Podgorać by a nostalgic contemporary torn between traditional ties to religion and the childish trance aroused in him by the celluloid demon of cinematography. Here are his words: *He was of tall stature (over six feet tall), black hair and deep black eyes. He was beautiful like the Hollywood actor Clark Gable, but instead of sensuality his eyes and smile reflected intelligence, spirituality, and kindness . . .*

And although he spent these four years mostly in study and meditation, one event confirms the fact that he remained true to his obsessive ideas. At the end of 1936, Father Tomislav, dressed as a miner, spent a month with Yugoslav miners in Belgian mines in a desire to feel on his own skin the life of the proletariat and to learn, in contact with miners, on an equal footing as a worker with other workers, about their relationship with religion and God. Some of the miners' faces called to mind some men he had known previously. With his first calluses he perhaps learned all the subconscious pragmatics of his decision to join the Jesuits. He must have understood, too, that among miners one cannot think about God as a metaphysical concept. A miner will, on demand and without excessive personal involvement, either praise or blaspheme God for anyone who can guarantee him a better life and security. But God is still deep in the human soul. Because even miners who openly declared themselves atheists would cry out when in trouble, as if by instinct: *God, help me!*

It is not reliably known where Tomislav Podgorać was between 1937 and 1940, and precisely that time represents the beginning of his famous mysteriousness. Nevertheless, it can be determined fairly reliably that he was in Spain during the Civil War and that he fought on the side of the Republicans. Selim Efendić testifies that some *compadre priest of ours* fought for the Spanish Republic. According to his words, that priest told him that the Republican slogan *No passaran* was in fact a quote from the Gospels. And in fact in the twenty-first chapter of the Gospel according to Luke it says: *Verily I say to you, this generation will not pass away till all has taken place. Heaven and earth will pass away, but my words will not pass away.*

In the summer of 1940 Tomislav Podgorać was in Zagreb again. He could often be seen in the company of the English consul Rapp, but he was equally often in bars in peripheral working-class districts where he agitated for *Christian socialism.* He founded the Workers Christian Socialist Movement with a group of young metal workers. Zagreb vicars were not really enamored of the young Jesuit. The malicious phrase *Podgorać likes cheap sour Zagorje wine better than sacramental wine* is still remembered. At the meetings of the Zagreb committee of the Communist Party at that time, activists complained that some priest was preaching to the sympathizers, telling them that there was no equality among people without equality before God. From that time on Father Podgorać would be under the vigilant surveillance of agents of the Communist Party, but soon much more dangerous days would come both for the communists and for Podgorać, and they would temporarily find themselves on the same side.

According to certain statements Father Podgorać already pointed to the danger of Nazism in Belgium in the mid-thirties. That almost legendary Spanish episode of his represents just an additional confirmation. But it is certainly known that at the end of 1940 and the beginning of 1941 in his bar preaching he constantly warned of the dangers threatening from Nazi Germany. The fulfillment of his sinister prophecies was an additional prod for him to fight against—as he used to say—*the worse monster.* It would be difficult to reconstruct all the details of his underground activity among workers and students to undermine belief in the empty phrases of the fascist authorities. In one note of the Ustasha's educational headquarters from 1942 it says: *Podgorać is a fiend who works among the Catholics against the NDH.*[2] Toward the end of that year the Gestapo and the Ustasha police issued an official arrest warrant for Tomislav Podgorać. For two months Father Tomislav moved around in civilian clothes and hid in friends' apartments. After the war he used to say that during those two months he did not spend more than three nights under the same roof. By Christmas of 1942, running just ahead of the Gestapo and the police, he arrived in Split, and at the beginning of the next year he was already in the Vatican.

It seems that Tomislav Podgorać was disappointed in the Jesuit Order, because after only three months spent in the Vatican he asked for a discharge and a transfer to the regular priesthood. It seems that the Vatican Jesuits considered Father Podgorać a camouflaged communist agent, though they only accused him openly of *leftist Catholicism.* But the provincial of the Society of Jesus, Grimm, did not give Podgorać a discharge, and so he addressed Pope Pius XII. The pope gave him an audience in mid-June. Although protocol did not allow for more than an hour, Tomislav Podgorać talked to the pope for more than three. Perhaps he captivated him with his fascinating eloquence and rhetorical talent. According to one cardinal's statement, nobody had ever so impressed the pope. Most of all, Father Podgorać did not approach the pope as Peter's infallible vicar. He attacked the passivity and indolence of the church in the Soviet Union, and expressed the fear that after the war, if things continued as they were, the atheistic Bolsheviks would reach the antechamber of the Vatican. When the holy father asked him what was to be done and who could change that, Father Tomislav said: *Me!* Then he set forth his ideas and plans. The pope only nodded. In parting he gave him a discharge from the Society of Jesus and a free hand for his *apostleship in the East* with an obligation to report to him regularly. Father Podgorać returned to Zagreb the next day.

In Zagreb, with help from the Slovakian consul, Tomislav Podgorać obtained a false identification with the name of Stjepan Kolaković. Kolaković was his mother's maiden name. In the document it said that his profession was physician. With this new identity he began a trip to Bratislava. The origin of his medical knowledge is unknown, but it is reliably known that on the way to Bratislava he saved the life of a wounded German soldier. In Slovakia Podgorać started to prepare the priests for action under an atheistic regime. Parishioners wondered about the pope's envoy, doubting his provenance, but later they would create a legend about *the father who had foreseen Yalta.* Tomislav Podgorać, alias Stjepan Kolaković, soon joined a Slovakian partisan unit that issued him the rank of medical captain. During his military days this self-proclaimed doctor purportedly completed dozens of surgeries without any mortality. One of his appendix operations, carried out in a forest clearing without anesthesia, became a legend. When the Red Army entered Slovakia, Father Podgorać, along with a few other priests, handed out two hundred thousand pictures of the Mother of God with an appropriate Russian text. When one of priest expressed doubts as to the utility of such an activity, Podgorać—according to the memory of this modern doubting Thomas—spoke like this: *The fundamental battle for or against God is not fought in doctrine but in human souls. No cruelty could rip the faith from the soul of a Russian. Churches are not important. The English word* temple *means both temple and tabernacle. That is not accidental. Nothing is accidental in language. The forehead is an altar, the eyes are colorful stained glass, the temples are supporting walls. The human head is the only true temple.*

At the beginning of 1945 Tomislav Podgorać arrived in the Soviet Union. He walked Moscow's boulevards in workers' clothing and talked to people. Supposedly, he inquired about the fate of Antun Mavrak. He converted several prominent Russian families to Catholicism. It seemed that Father Podgorać believed that time would inevitably lead to the abandonment of dogmatic godlessness. He often said that he dreamed about a Russia in which the socialist movement would remain, but atheism would be abandoned. In the fall of that same year he went to the Vatican from Moscow. One Jesuit periodical wrote that the pope welcomed him with a smile and a question: *Is it true, Father, that you are a Slovak now?* Certain circles are inclined to overestimate Podgorać's influence on Pius XII. These insinuations go as far as to suggest that the pope declared the dogma about the bodily assumption of the Virgin Mary because of Podgorać's conviction that the cult of the Virgin Mary in the East was somewhat more central than that of the Holy Trinity and that such a dogma would firm up faith in countries under the Bolshevik boot. From Rome he traveled to Prague with the task of renewing the lay movement of Catholic Action, but the communist authorities there arrested him. In jail, Podgorać gave sermons both to the prisoners and the guards. After intervention by the French embassy he was freed. Tomislav Podgorać spent roughly another year traveling around Czechoslovakia and Poland, getting to know many people, among them the recent seminary graduate Karol Woytila. At the end of 1946 in a Red Cross train, in a car for typhus patients, Father Tomislav went from Prague to Belgium.

From that time the life of Father Tomislav Podgorać again entered a kind of dark period comparable to that just before World War II. But this era of mystery would last much longer, in fact it would last almost until Father Tomislav's death. According to the research of a certain American woman who published a book, *God's Underground,* about Father Podgorać, he used nine false names in one seven-year period, having the same number of professions in that time. Among others, he was a doctor, a professor, a locksmith, and a sewer worker. His dossier in one of the Yugoslav security services characterizes him in the following way: *Dr. Tomislav Podgorać is an unusually intelligent, capable organizer, and ready for any kind of action. It is reliably known that he speaks French, Italian, German, English, Russian, Czech, Slovak, and Polish, and most likely he uses Chinese and some Indian languages. He knows ancient Greek, Latin, and Hebrew extraordinarily well. He changes clothes as necessary, now into civilian garb, now into that of a priest. He constantly changes residences, but it could be said that Paris is his base. He uses the pseudonyms Kolaković, Father George, Houang . . .*

Most likely Tomislav Podgorać resided primarily in Belgium until the beginning of the fifties. The early fifties took him, it appears, to the Far East, to China and India. Contradictory information about him arrived from China. One source says that Tomislav Podgorać alias Houang organized a guerrilla group and that a large bounty for his head was announced, like in the Wild West. According to other, seemingly more reliable sources, Podgorać was the closest collaborator of Cardinal Cardijn, the founder of the Joeistes. Father Podgorać considered the idea of spreading the Joeiste movement around the world, of its internationalization.

In India Podgorać appears to have led a Christian commune, a farm on which he perhaps tried locally to turn some of his global ideas into reality. With him as missionaries there were, it is said, some of his former students from Travnik. But it seems that the climate did not suit Father Tomislav's ruined health. After a heart attack, he was treated in a Calcutta hospital. He was unconscious for several days. When he regained consciousness he suffered a temporary amnesia; he forgot his name and all languages except his native one. He cried: *Vode! Vode!*[3] Mother Theresa understood him. Perhaps Agnez Gonxha Bojaxhiu remembered her childhood.

At the end of the fifties and the beginning of the sixties Father Tomislav seemed to slow down. It is known that in Paris in 1958 he led an intensive course on Christian theology. One of the students was from his homeland, and he, in her words, wanted to show her his apartment. But he drove her for hours through labyrinths of tiny Parisian streets so that she did not even know what arrondissement she was in. She thought he did this not simply out of a desire for mystery, but rather it seemed to her that *Father Tomislav simply enjoyed the drive.* He told her he had worked as a cab driver for a while. Podgorać, it seemed, frequently changed cars, because those whom he drove could not agree on what type of car he drove. But it was always black with tinted windows, and they all agreed that he drove *devilishly fast*. Besides Paris, he was seen in America and in the Vatican during the sixties. In the fall of 1961 he was in Oslo and Stockholm. It seems that on one occasion he had breakfast with Kennedy. He participated in preparations for the Second Vatican Council. Some sources also note his influence on some of the council's decisions. It is said that in the seventies Father Tomislav was often in Ireland. He was almost completely alone. He read a lot. According to some indications, he wrote a lot, too, but it seems that before his death he carried out a version of Kafka's will for himself. In the eighties he was purportedly seen again in Poland and Czechoslovakia, but it is more probable that these are the speculations of those *conspiracy theorists* who see the fingers of Father Tomislav Podgorać everywhere.

Tomislav Podgorać died in 1990 in Paris (*if he died at all*, as it says in one newspaper hagiography), and I (I who wrote this) am now asking myself who was the man with whom I talked in the grove behind the high school in the spring of 1989, Anno Domini. I was twelve. I was walking beneath the just budding chestnut trees. I liked to climb those trees. The grove was always deserted—the ideal place for a lonely boy to play. But this morning an old man in a frock coat was sitting on one of the stumps. He was smoking and smiling silently. On the left side of his chest, at heart level, he had a red flower stuck into his buttonhole.

It's not May 1.—I said with childish arrogance.

It's not, but Easter comes in seven days, and the resurrected lamb will be crucified again on May 1.—the stranger replied. *What is your name?*—he asked.

Muharem.—I said. *And yours?*

You'd be better off asking what it isn't.—he said with a quiet laugh. He stayed silent for a bit and then added: *You look like someone, Muharem. I've seen a lot of people.* Then he removed the flower from his frock and offered it to me: *Take this and may God be with you.*

I turned around and went down toward the school building (then it was still called *Antun Mavrak High School*). The grove in fact is on a very steep slope and you must walk down carefully. Something tempted me to turn around, but I could not. I ran down in thirty seconds or so and looked back toward the grove. There was nobody on the stump. Thick bluish streaks floated in the air, it could have been cigarette smoke, but also fog. I thought I had dreamed it, but in my hand there was a flower.

■ □ ■ □ ■

AUTHOR'S NOTE

The stories of *The Second Book* are set in different epochs and happen at different locations; the vertical chronological line of *The Second Book* covers approximately three and a half millennia, or thirty-five centuries, while its geography includes among others Turin, Belgrade, Prague, Egypt, Calcutta, Paris, the Amazon, Cetinje, Istanbul, Venice, New York, and Travnik.

"Tears in Turin" is an attempt to depict the last few days of Nietzsche's life before his famous descent into madness. The inspiration for this variation, in addition to my own frequent reading of Nietzsche's works, came primarily from two rather disparate authors: Milan Kundera and Jim Morrison. In the last section of *The Unbearable Lightness of Being* Milan Kundera says in one place:

Another image also comes to mind: Nietzsche leaving his hotel in Turin. Seeing a horse and a coachman beating it with a whip, Nietzsche went up to the horse and, before the coachman's very eyes, put his arms around the horse's neck and burst into tears.

In the first edition of his first book *The Lords* Morrison devoted one section to Nietzsche. It is interesting that this section along with two others was omitted from all subsequent editions of this book. The section starts with this paragraph:

On the third of January, near the door of his lodgings, Nietzsche saw a cabman whipping a horse. He threw his arms around the animal's neck and burst into tears, marking the first hour of his madness.

These few sentences were Dženetić's grain of sand for this story.

"The Poet" was imagined as a short Borgesian hybrid half-story–half-essay based on a topic that I once jotted down under the codename *poet-Muslim*. The story was supposed to be written based on the pattern *The Life and Work of Such and Such a Person,* where in the form of an obituary there are set forth very shortly his life and finally the thesis that he sacrificed his life as the least important element from the triptych *life-work-belief.* But when I thought about where I could set the story, I realized that by setting it in Bosnia I could enrich the story many times without losing anything of its original idea. The initial motif was of course the Koran's position about poets whose essence I knew from memory. But when I looked for the specific lines to take them for the story's epigraph I realized that I would have to *break off* the quote. Because after the condemnation of the poets quoted in the epigraph, the Koran goes on to say:

Except those who believe, and do good deeds,
and remember Allah frequently,
and who resist
when injustice is done to them!

I was compelled, therefore, to use a truncated quotation for the epigraph, because only in such a way did it express the spirit and fundamental thought of the story or the letter of Dženetić's friend. The comma that ends the epigraph is there as a hint at that truncation. Meša Selimović did something similar in his novel *Death and the Dervish* when, after the beginning lines from the chapter El-'asr,

I call to witness time, the beginning and end
of all things—to witness that every man always suffers loss.

he left out the continuation of the quote:

Except those who believe and do good deeds
and who proffer the truth!

He even added a period instead of a comma, suggesting a completed thought. In one interview in 1972 Selimović says:

In the introductory epigraph of Death and the Dervish *I cut off the Koranic quote, but its sense, in my opinion a broader one, is in the context of the whole novel . . . In this sense I did not betray the Koran.*

I believe the same is true for "The Poet," but nevertheless I left the comma in the epigraph as a hint to the careful reader.

As for Amenhotep IV or Akhenaton, the damned pharaoh, the hero of the story *The Hot Sun's Golden Circle,* I heard of him for the first time as a twelve-year-old when I read the famous comic *The Mystery of the Great Pyramid* by Edgar P. Jacobs. That character has fascinated me ever since. Freud's discussion of *Moses—the Egyptian* only deepened that fascination whose product is this story. On the basis of the Koran's position that in the Book the names of messengers are not mentioned, Mustafa Mahmood turns the Freudian thesis around somewhat, and proposes that Akhenaton was a messenger. *Egyptian Mythology* by Veronica Ions helped the plausibility of Akhenaton's rhetoric. The title of the story comes from an unknown monk of the eighteenth century, and I got it via Andrić. In fact, one of *his signs along the road* reads like this:

More about language. About how, through decades and centuries language took shape, transformed, and developed on the road toward ever-greater clarity, beauty, and perfection. In one of our anthologies of poetry there is a poem by an unknown monk of the eighteenth century in which he complains that his ascetic destiny deprives him of all of life's joys and pleasantries. In that poem the language is poor, the verse doggerel, the rhymes off. But even in such a poem somewhere a verse shines through, clear as a dewdrop under the sun, and its shine foretells how well our poets would be able and capable of writing in that same language sometime in the future. For example, this verse:

The hot sun's golden circle . . .

And today, whenever I read that verse, it seems to me that I see, and not only see but hear, too, how a young creature, alive and joyful, jumps on invisible stairs made of pure light.

The first version of "A Twilight Encounter" was published in the magazine *Divan* in November 1995. The basic reason that I included a somewhat revised version in this collection is that Wilkinson (as I quote in the section "The Final Note") is truly mentioned in a footnote of *The Second Book* of Schopenhauer's *The World as Will and Representation,* and so I later found the connection between this story and the book named after the story *The Second Book.* The other reason is mentioned in the last fragment, the section titled "*Postscriptum.*" Only Krleža's phrase from the essay

"Behind the Scenes of the Year 1918" could stand as the epigraph to this story:

a head on a Turkish stake or a Turkish head in front of Biljarda.

"The Story of Two Brothers" was created as a somewhat essayistic analysis of a particular realization of an eternal biblical topic. The same topic is at the foundation of, among others: Borges's story "The Interloper" and poem "The Two Brothers Milonga"; Joyce's novel *Finnegans Wake;* the movies *East of Eden* and *Paris, Texas;* and Ry Cooder's instrumental music "Brothers."

The story called "Fiat Iustitia" represents a somewhat postmodernist game with the number thirty-six, a Hasidic legend, and a Latin proverb. Rereading Kundera's "Dialogue on the Art of Composition" after this story had already been written, I realized that it almost perfectly satisfied the requirements of what Kundera calls polyphony. That is to say that in this story several formally different lines interact with one another: verses (for example, Borges's poems), narrative (the story about Albert and Daniel), and an essay about justice (and precisely the kind of essay that Kundera considers suitable to fit into a novel or a story—an essay *that does not strive to bring an apodictic message but rather remains hypothetical, ludic, or ironic*). All these lines are united, of course, by the topic of the number thirty-six and the legend of the thirty-six just men. Kundera insists on the equality of the lines, and that equality is ensured here—truly magically—by the special nature of number thirty-six, as it is interpreted in the story. Another strange discovery happened after the story was written. Looking through some old things, I stumbled upon a textbook of painting for elementary schools by Željko Filipović published by *Svjetlost* in 1990. Randomly leafing through it, I noticed a reproduction of the engraving *Ritter, tod und teufel* as an example of etching technique. But I went numb when I saw above the reproduction the title *Knight, Death, and the Scales.* Where did that error in translation come from, I asked myself (the phonetic similarity of the words *vrag*[1] and *vaga*[2] in the Bosnian language, perhaps), and is it possible that some imprint in my brain prodded me to remember this engraving in the context of the scales and justice? Apropos the specific relationship between the poet and the number thirty-six it should be said that Joyce's *Chamber Music* is composed of thirty-six poems.

"The Second Book," of course, is the title story. It is related to *The Library of Babel* and *The Encyclopedia of the Dead.* In some Hegelian context it perhaps represents their synthesis. *The Library of Babel* was published when Kiš was six years old, *The Encyclopedia of the Dead* when I was six years old.

"The Bridge on Land" was written as a product of triple inspiration. The first is symbolized in the epigraph to this story, taken from Calvino's *Invisible Cities.* That is, thus, the vision of Mehmed as the new Ulysses, his war trick as a new Trojan horse, Constantinople as the new Troy (especially in the context of the fact that its citizens—according to the legend from the *Aeneid*—were in fact descendants of the Trojan refugees). Constantinople is often called *kuduz-elma* (golden apple). Is it necessary to mention that a golden apple was the original cause of the Trojan war. At the same time, "The Bridge on Land" is a kind of an antistory to Andrić's *The Bridge on the Žepa.* Vizier Jusef is a *Homo poeticus,* Mehmed is a *homo politicus;* this of course reflects on their bridges. This allusion to *The Bridge on the Žepa* is made more visible by some—as people like to say today—postmodernist twitch—like quotes. *And last but not least* there is the historical coincidence that the first mention of Travnik in history (June 3, 1463) comes exactly ten years and four days after Mehmed's conquest of Istanbul (May 29, 1453), and that mention concerns the fact that Mehmed conquered Travnik also. This is more than enough for a literary game (historically based) that brings Mehmed to the walls of Travnik for the first time exactly ten years after he conquered Constantinople. It is also interesting to mention that in one of his works, perhaps in error, Joseph Kosuth gives as the date of the conquest of Constantinople May 29, 1463, moving the real date ten years ahead (an error on the gravestone of the builder Sinan, the architect of the bridge on the Drina, also moves the date of his death ten years ahead). Still this May 29, 1463, or June 3, 1463, is not any less important than May 29, 1453.

The subtitle of "The Threshold of Maturity" could be the title of a story by the hero of "The Story of Two Brothers"; that is the title of a story by Henry James: "Four Meetings." Its hero Pavel runs away from *laughable loves.* The mention of Australia spreads out the map of "The Second Book" to that continent as well. Pavel's character is most clearly shown by his artistic affinities. Pavel and Mihaela considered "Hand in Glove" by the Smiths to be their song. If young lovers were not so careful to avoid mentioning the end, it could have happened that they would have loved the song "Dance Me to the End of Love" by Leonard Cohen:

Touch me with your naked hand
Touch me with your glove
Dance me to the end of love.

"A Red Flower for Tomislav Podgorać" is a biography that in a Maupassantian way (*une vie*) tries to fix the adventure of the twentieth century. Tomislav Podgorać is a police sketch of Tomislav Poglajen. The last name Podgorać was based on the examples by Dominquez-Domenico Palermo, Vito Corleone, or Mehmed Soković; that is, in fact, the name of the village, in the story unnamed, near Našice. The story follows the facts from that Jesuit's biography pretty faithfully. So much has been written about the relationship between Christianity and communism, Podgorać's obsession, that this topic can be, without a lot of exaggeration, considered one of the great topics of the twentieth century. For example, Czesław Miłosz (*The Captive Mind, Native Realm*), Maria Vargas Llosa (*The Real Life of Alejandro Mayta*), Italo Calvino (*The Watcher*), Jorge Semprun, Bertrand Russell, and George Steiner touched upon it. Multiple inspiration is again responsible for the title of the story: one thought comes from the symbolic meanings of roses and carnations, the elegance of roses and the ordinariness of carnations; there is also the title of Andrić's story "The Red Flower," and a photograph of the band U2 in which Bono holds a red flower that is either a rose or a carnation. At the end of the story an allusion to Coleridge can, of course, be discovered. But even after the completion of this story *La part de Dieu* (or *La part de diable*) happened. In Bakhtin's *Problems of Dostoyevsky's Poetics* I discovered this little-known quote—from Dostoyevsky's notebooks:

The definition of morality as loyalty to one's own convictions is insufficient. A person should always ask himself the question: are my convictions right? There is only one touchstone—Christ. But this is no longer philosophy, it is religion, and religion is a red flower . . .

I write this epilogue, some kind of hybrid of the epilogue, the *postscriptum,* and what is, in the Anglo-Saxon world, called *acknowledgments* after *The Second Book* won the award by the Open Society of Bosnia and Herzegovina (better known as the Soros award) as the best book of stories published in 1999. Books for the contest were considered anonymously. I mention this just because of the fact that the code name under which the manuscript was submitted explains a somewhat obscure allusion at the very end of the book. There, a twelve-year-old who liked to climb trees is mentioned. Ten years later that twelve-year-old signed the manuscript of *The Second Book* with the code name *Cosimo.* That name recalls, of course, the best known twelve-year-old ever to climb trees: Cosimo Piovasco di Rondo; *the baron in the trees.*

Translated from the Bosnian by Oleg Andrić and Andrew Wachtel

■ □ ■ □ ■

TRANSLATORS' NOTES

The Poet

1. Religiously educated men, learned men, especially in a religious sense.

2. A judge of the religious law of Islam.

3. An honorific title; someone who knows the Koran by heart.

4. Priests in Islam.

5. Learned men.

6. Islamic religious law.

7. Islamic religious secondary school.

8. Vlachs or Wallachs, an ethnic minority in the Balkans; used disparagingly to describe those not belonging to the majority Muslim culture.

9. Friday's prayer.

10. Evening prayer announcing the start of Ramadan (Eid al Fitr).

11. An Iranian poem with four half-verses.

12. The Communist Party.

13. Better war than the pact.

14. The Turkish name for Venice also used in Bosnia.

15. Another Bosnian name for the Republic of Venice.

16. Mystics who concerned themselves mainly with the purification of the soul.

17. The Ramadan breakfast after sunset.

The Hot Sun's Golden Circle

1. The act of Mohammed of taking his followers from Mecca to Medina.

Fiat Iustitia

1. Translated by Alastair Reid.
2. Translated by Stephen Kessler.

The Second Book

1. Ambiguity (Latin).
2. Translated by Rev. Charles C. Starbuck, Andover, Mass.

The Threshold of Maturity

1. Masking of the true belief behind a facade of conformity to the new regime in communist countries.

A Red Flower for Tomislav Podgorać

1. Islamic religious secondary school.
2. Independent State of Croatia.
3. Water! Water!

Author's Note

1. Devil.
2. Scales.

Muharem Bazdulj was born in Travnik (Bosnia) in 1977. He graduated in English and American studies from the University of Sarajevo. One of the leading writers of the younger generation from ex-Yugoslavia, he has published three books of short stories and one novel. He is also a playwright, a journalist, an essayist, and the translator of a collection of selected poems by Joseph Brodsky from English to Bosnian.

Andrew Wachtel is the dean of the Graduate School at Northwestern University and a professor of Slavic languages and literatures. He is the editor of *Intersections and Transpositions: Russian Music, Literature, and Society* and *Petrushka: Sources and Contexts*, both published by Northwestern University Press.

Oleg Andrić was born and raised in Sarajevo. Since 1992, he has been living in Florida. Although an electrical engineer by trade, he finds enjoyment in translating from the language in which he dreams to the language in which he lives.

■ □ ■ □ ■

WRITINGS FROM AN UNBOUND EUROPE

For a complete list of titles, see the Writings from an Unbound Europe Web site at www.nupress.northwestern.edu/ue.

Tsing
Words Are Something Else
DAVID ALBAHARI

Perverzion
YURI ANDRUKHOVYCH

The Second Book
MUHAREM BAZDULJ

Skinswaps
ANDREJ BLATNIK

The Grand Prize and Other Stories
DANIELA CRĂSNARU

Peltse and Pentameron
VOLODYMYR DIBROVA

The Tango Player
CHRISTOPH HEIN

A Bohemian Youth
JOSEF HIRŠAL

Mocking Desire
DRAGO JANČAR

A Land the Size of Binoculars
IGOR KLEKH

Balkan Blues: Writing Out of Yugoslavia
EDITED BY JOANNA LABON

The Loss
VLADIMIR MAKANIN

Compulsory Happiness
NORMAN MANEA

Zenobia
GELLU NAUM

Border State
TÕNU ÕNNEPALU

How to Quiet a Vampire: A Sotie
BORISLAV PEKIĆ

A Voice: Selected Poems
ANZHELINA POLONSKAYA

Merry-Making in Old Russia and Other Stories
EVGENY POPOV

Estonian Short Stories
EDITED BY KAJAR PRUUL AND DARLENE REDDAWAY

Death and the Dervish
The Fortress
MEŠA SELIMOVIĆ

House of Day, House of Night
OLGA TOKARCZUK

Materada
FULVIO TOMIZZA

Fording the Stream of Consciousness
DUBRAVKA UGREŠIĆ

Shamara and Other Stories
SVETLANA VASILENKO

The Silk, the Shears and *Marina; or, About Biography*
IRENA VRKLJAN